JACK

◇ ◇ ◇

A. M. HOMES

◇ ◇ ◇

MACMILLAN PUBLISHING COMPANY   NEW YORK

The author would like to thank James A. Michener and the Copernicus Society of America, the New York Foundation for the Arts, the Henfield Foundation, and the Edward Albee Foundation for their generous support.

And special thanks to Eric Ashworth, Alice Turner, and Randall Kenan for their patience and humor.

◇　　　◇　　　◇

Excerpt from the song "Me and Bobby McGee" by Kris Kristofferson and Fred Foster copyright © 1969 Combine Music Corporation. All Rights Controlled and Administered by SBK Blackwood Music Inc. All Rights Reserved. International Copyright Secured. Used by Permission.

10   9   8   7   6   5   4   3   2   1

The text of this book is set in 11 point Sabon.

Library of Congress Cataloging-in-Publication Data • Homes, A. M. Jack / by A. M. Homes. — 1st ed.   p.   cm. Summary: Fifteen-year-old Jack's confused feelings for his father, who left him and his mother four years earlier, are further complicated when he finds that his father is gay.

ISBN 0-02-744831-2

[1. Fathers and sons—Fiction. 2. Homosexuality—Fiction.] I. Title.

PZ7.H7453Jac   1989   [Fic]—dc19   89-31061   CIP   AC

◇   ◇   ◇

To my parents,
my brother,
and my Grummama

◇   ◇   ◇

"**B**e careful," my father said before I'd even taken my foot off the brake.

"We don't have to do this," I said. "I can wait and get my license when I'm thirty—no problem. I can get Vernon, my driving teacher, to give me extra lessons."

"This time, cut the wheel the other way before you ease up on the pedal."

I turned the steering wheel as far as I could. The old blue Volvo didn't believe in power steering.

"More," my father said.

I thought I would die. I thought I might have a heart attack. I thought if I ever had to drive that car, I'd end up looking like Arnold Schwarzenegger.

"I think I'm having a heart attack," I said.

"What?"

"Never mind."

I saw him in the rearview mirror. I could see him in the mirror attached to the door. I turned my head around so I could look out the back window. He was standing there, leaning on one leg. His thumbs were hooked through the loops of his jeans. His hair was long and needed cutting. He stood there, not really looking like my father. He looked younger. He looked like a guy, just standing there, waiting. I stepped down on the gas, hard, and felt the car fly backward. I felt the steering wheel unwind in my hands. It was like the burn you get from flying a kite and letting out the string too fast.

My father jumped out of the way, his fingers unhooked from his belt loops. The wheels went up and over the curb. The rear bumper smashed into a tree, and then the car rolled a little bit forward, catching on the curb.

"Are you all right?" I yelled out the window.

"What did you do that for?" my father asked.

I shrugged. A car isn't a car, I thought to myself, it's a machine.

"It wasn't exactly planned," I said. "Should I try again?"

He picked up the orange pylons and threw them into the trunk. Guess not, I thought.

"Why don't we call it a day," he said.

I wanted to drive. I wanted to keep going, forward. I wanted to break out onto the highway, put my foot to the floor, turn on the radio, and sing along.

"I can drive," I said. "I mean, I do have my learner's."

"I know," my father said. "But I can't teach you. I just can't."

I slid across to the passenger side. My shirt stuck to the driver's seat, and then it pulled away with a soft sucking sound.

"Jack, don't get me wrong. I'm just not a teacher."

He pulled out onto the parkway. He didn't spin his head around like Linda Blair in *The Exorcist*. He didn't look in all forty directions at once, the way Vernon said you should.

"Maybe we can try again in a couple of days," he said. "It's just the parallel parking that seems to be a problem. We can work on it."

I pulled the visor down and looked at myself in the clip-on mirror. My face floated, weightless, unmarked. The skin was clean and white, with freckles. My face floated, unlike my father's, which seemed thick and heavy, broken by the lines around his mouth and eyes.

"So, how's Mom?" he asked.

"Okay."

"And school?"

"The same."

"Max?"

I nodded. It was his checklist. Every time we were together we went through this. He ran down his list of people, events, even actual objects that were in my life.

"Basketball?"

"The garden's doing real well, and I think Max is getting back to sort of normal." I said it all at once to save him the trouble of having to hit on each thing, one at a time.

He smiled. "Good."

We were quiet.

"When you're ready, I want to take you to get your license."

"That's okay. Michael said he would. His car is smaller anyway."

I flipped the visor back up into the ceiling.

"I want to, Jack. Is that all right?"

He reached across the car, swept my hair off my face, and rubbed my cheek with the back of his hand.

"Yeah, sure, we'll see," I said.

"How about dinner Wednesday?" he asked as he pulled up in front of our house.

I nodded.

"We'll go someplace nice, just you and me. Pick you up around seven."

"Yeah, okay. See you," I said as I got out.

He put the car in gear and pulled away without checking his mirrors. Luckily, nothing was coming.

I worry about him. Sometimes I'm not sure his receiver is on the hook, if you know what I mean.

I watched the blue Volvo creep down the street and wondered how I'd ever get it to fit in the goddamned parallel-parking place at the Motor Vehicle Administration.

"Salvation Army's coming tomorrow," Michael said when I walked into the kitchen. He was chopping vegetables with something that looked like the ax George Washington must have used when he cut down his cherry tree.

"Get whatever you don't want and put it out front."

I made myself a Muenster-cheese sandwich, with lettuce, tomato, mustard, and mayo, and went up to my room. Ingredients are important.

The entire top shelf of my closet was filled with stuff; historical artifacts of my entire life before this moment, old clothes, dead stuffed animals, notebooks, projects. It was all there, like I was saving it just in case for my sixteenth birthday the Smithsonian decided to do an exhibit on me. I pulled out crucial elements, things I would need in case I ever got amnesia and had to be reminded of who I was. The rest of it, all of it, I dumped into a huge box. I didn't even go through the stuff. Being one of those saver types, I knew if I stopped to look, to actually handle things, I'd be sitting on the floor of my room until I was thirty and the Salvation Army had come and gone, completely.

Just before I carried the box downstairs, I turned off the lamp on my desk, unplugged it, and stuffed it way down in the box, a little concerned because the bulb was still hot and I imagined it starting a fire that would be incredibly difficult to explain. There was absolutely nothing wrong with the lamp, but I unplugged that flashlight on a leash and shoved it right in there with the blue-and-green flannel shirt I wore every day during the winter of sixth grade and the Roy Rogers personally autographed cowboy hat someone bought me at a circus two hundred years ago. I realize it was slightly insane, but for the longest time I was convinced that the lamp was totally responsible for my family falling apart and my whole life getting wrecked. I know my life wasn't really wrecked, only slightly dented, and the lamp had nothing to do with it. All the same, I had the feeling that a part of me would never be all right until that lamp was gone. And I mean gone. I couldn't just put it in the basement or something. It had to go in a big way, hauled off by four guys with a Salvation Army truck.

As far as I could tell, that particular lamp was in my room on the day I was born, because I have no memory of it arriving after me. But the night it left comes back like it was tattooed on my brain. I was maybe eleven years old, lying in bed wearing the fifty-percent-cotton-fifty-percent-polyester guaranteed-never-to-get-comfortable pajamas my grandmother had just sent me, and my father came in to say good-night. He leaned against my desk and picked up the model airplane I'd spent all afternoon gluing.

Even in the wicked, disgusting sweats he put on every day after work, he looked like a movie star. It isn't the kind of stuff a kid normally says about his dad, but it was true; there was just something about him, a weird kind of confidence that made everyone turn around and look.

"Do you use this lamp?" he asked, turning the switch around and around like a maniac so the lamp kept flashing off and on, switching my room back and forth from night to day, like a special effect.

"I dunno, why?"

"I was thinking of using it in the other room."

"You have a lamp."

"I left it for Mommy. Can I borrow yours?"

"I guess," I said.

I guess, I said, like what am I, an idiot?

He moved into the other bedroom and then he moved out.

One Saturday morning a couple of months after he borrowed the lamp, my father went to the grocery store. He got milk, orange juice, bread, all the regular things, and he got boxes. He put the food in the refrigerator and started packing. All his things from the bathroom cabinet went into the shoe box that my new loafers had come out of the week before. He even went through the big wicker hamper in the bathroom, picking out his dirty clothes and throwing them into one of those giant green trashbags along with all his clean stuff, like he didn't know what the hell he was doing.

Before he left, he brought the lamp back into my room, put it down on the desk, and plugged it in.

"Are we going to the movie?" I said.

It wasn't what I wanted to say, but it was all that would come out. I was sitting at my desk gluing a tall ship.

"I have to move some stuff."

The mainmast came off in my hand and stayed glued to my thumb and first finger.

"I want to go to the movies."

To be honest, I didn't give a damn about the movie, but there was something horrible going on and I didn't know what it was and I didn't know what to do, except act normal. We'd gone to the movies every week since I was about three.

"It's Saturday. We go to the movies on Saturday."

Normally I'm a movie freak. In fact, I am a movie. It's always me out there in a medium close-up. It's like there's a camera on me, trailing me, getting down every move. A long, slow, tracking shot of my life.

I pulled the mast off my fingers. It went back and forth, first sticking to my thumb and then to my other finger, and finally the balsa wood snapped, the glue started to dry and I managed to pull the mast off and follow my dad downstairs.

"I'm pretty well packed," my dad said when he walked into the kitchen.

My mother squeezed some Ivory soap into a dirty pot and turned on the water.

"Jack wants to go to the movies. I thought I'd drop off the stuff and then take him."

She rinsed the pot, put it down on the drainboard, and wiped her hands on a dish towel. My mother looked at my dad for a minute, then tilted her head back, ran her long skinny fingers through her long brown hair, and said, "You're not taking him anywhere, ever." She took a cigarette from her pocket and lit it. Smoke curled up and around her face.

"What?" my father said.

"I mean it, Paul." She took a big drag and started coughing.

"He wants to go to the movies," he said. "It's Saturday. We go to the movies on Saturdays."

I pressed my gluey fingers together and pulled them apart over and over again. They worked like magnets, sticking together and then snapping apart.

"I'll take him," she said.

She crossed her arms in front of her chest. The ash from her cigarette fell onto the floor. My dad looked down at it, but she pretended nothing had happened.

They stood there, staring at each other, swelling up the whole room. I remember the sudden strange sensation that these were not my parents, these were not the same people I'd known last week.

"You're acting extreme," my father said.

"Don't even begin to tell me how I'm acting," my mother said.

Everything looked the same, but during the night something from another planet, or maybe another house down the street, had come in and taken over my parents' bodies.

"Fine, fine," my father said, backing up until he was almost out the front door. "No movie today, Jackie."

"Why not?"

The stickiness had worn off, and my fingers were stiff with dried glue.

"Because I said so," my mother yelled.

Then she turned around and ran back through the house, out the kitchen door, and into the garden.

"I'm real sorry about this," my dad said, looking down at my untied shoelaces.

I shrugged. "It's just a movie."

"I have to leave," he said. "I'll call you later."

He went over and knocked on one of the dining room windows to get my mother's attention. I could see her standing in the garden, looking at the tomato plants.

"I'm going," my dad screamed through the glass. His breath fogged up two panes. She didn't turn around. He hugged me and went out the front door, lugging the last two of the giant green trash bags.

A lot of things went out the door that day. Things we didn't notice until later, like the hammer.

"I don't want to be one of those women who says horrible things about her husband, but your father had no right to take the hammer. I had that hammer when we were still dating, and he damn well knew it."

Until then, I'd never thought of anything as belonging to my mother or father. I'd always assumed that everything belonged to us as a group. I mean, we were supposed to be a family.

When you're a kid and you've got a father who reminds you of Superman, who seems like he can do anything, a father who's the kind of guy that climbs up onto the roof to rescue your dweebe G I Joe when it gets stuck up there during some idiotic experiment, and then one day he's gone, totally disappeared into a million green plastic garbage bags, no explanations offered, nothing anyone says later makes a bit of difference.

It's like you had a hero and all of the sudden he's all gone. He's gone but it isn't over because the whole thing, the whole way it happened, makes you start questioning everything and wondering about everything and your whole life turns into this mess that hurts incredibly and you constantly try and explain it to yourself and anyone who might listen.

One of the most disgusting parts of the whole mess was how right after my dad left he kept coming back. Not for keeps or anything. In fact, he never set foot in the house. But sometimes, out of nowhere, he would just appear in the backyard and start watering the plants. Whenever my mom caught him, she would order me up to my room and start banging on the kitchen windows, yelling that when he left her it also meant he left the plants.

One afternoon, he pulled up with two other guys and a truckful of cement. They dug a deep hole in the dirt next to the driveway and started to sink the basketball pole we'd been talking about for three years. My mom shuffled out in a Mickey Mouse sweatshirt that almost came down to her knees, a pair of jeans, and my dad's old red wool ski socks.

"What are you doing?" she said, lighting a cigarette.

Sometimes it seemed like my mother couldn't do anything without lighting a cigarette first.

"Putting in a hoop for Jack."

I stood in the front door, watching, knowing my mom would shoot me if I even thought of stepping outside, and praying that she wouldn't make him stop. My dad's two friends stopped shoveling.

"Do it, then leave," she said, dropping her cigarette into the fresh cement and grinding it out with my dad's red sock.

She walked back toward the house, the cemented sock dragging slightly behind. She took the socks off at the door and threw them out into the middle of the front yard. As soon as she stepped inside, she turned around and ran barefoot back to where my dad and his friends were trying to straighten out the pole.

"Don't come back here again, all right. I don't want to see you in the front yard or the backyard or anywhere."

She yelled in his face while everyone watched. I felt like people from everywhere up and down the street, inside their houses, and maybe all the way to California could hear what was going on.

"It's my house, my garden. If the plants die, it's because I want them to. Got it?"

She started to walk away, and my dad turned back to what he was doing. Then, all of a sudden, she grabbed him by the shirt.

"And don't keep pulling stunts like this, because next time I won't let you get away with it."

My dad didn't say anything. He looked past my mother at me standing in the doorway. He waved. She slapped his hand down, came back into the house, and slammed the door.

In the cold part of the night, while my mother was on the phone with Elaine Burka, her best friend, I went outside. I looked at the basketball hoop I'd always wanted, and threw my weight against the pole again and again until the soft cement gave a little and the pole was forever tilted slightly to the left.

◇   ◇   ◇

My father was banned from the grounds. That's what my mother's lawyer called the lawn in the front and back of the house, "the grounds." It was illegal for him even to step on the grass without calling and getting permission from my mother. At first, he called every night. My mother would yell and scream at him for a half hour and then hang up before I even got a chance to say hello. Eventually, she laid down the law. No explanations offered. She said I wasn't going to see my father for a while and that he would only be allowed to call the house once a week. Even though I probably should have hated her for cutting him out, I was relieved. At least with my dad not sneaking in to water plants and my mother not crying all night every night, I could pretend things were normal.

The dial-a-dad program was a disaster. He would keep me on the phone forever, and as much as I wanted to say stuff, maybe even yell at him, all I really had was a white receiver in my hand. I would pace around the kitchen, wrapping the cord around myself, opening and closing everything—the cabinets, the refrigerator, the cookie jar. I could hear him trying to pull the words out of me. But a telephone wasn't the same as a father.

What really got me was the fact that he didn't even disappear to another city or something. I mean, I knew where he lived. I was the one who forwarded his mail. If I walked down to the subway station and caught a train, I could be three blocks from his apartment in about twenty minutes. And even though I knew my mom would put me in the microwave if she found out, I used to ride down there and stand across the street from his building. I thought that maybe when he came in or out, he'd see me, and somehow everything would be okay again.

I used to wait there, like a rock in the middle of the sidewalk. People would go around me and sometimes bump right into me, as if I didn't even exist. There were a million little kids that played in front of the building. They grew there, like moss. Everyone who came in or out said something to them. And then there was me, across the street, hovering like a goddamn psycho killer.

On account of playing warden and getting her lawyer to tell my dad what he could and couldn't do, my mother started feeling guilty for wrecking my life. So, she took it upon herself to become my new dad. Besides going to real-estate school and getting a job selling condos for one of those companies that advertises on TV and makes you wear a pea-green polyester jacket with their name sewn on the pocket, she learned how to play basketball.

I shouldn't say learned, because she already knew how. But she spent a lot of time practicing her lay-ups and foul shots so she could come to the park without totally embarrassing me.

"You know," she said one night after she'd beaten me in two out of three games of Horse, "I like this. Maybe I should be on a team."

"Like the Celtics," I said.

I hated the Celtics. They were all height and no soul.

"No, something at the rec department."

I remember her dribbling the ball all the way home. She kept it low, close to the ground, switching back and forth hand to hand, never fumbling.

Right around then, besides turning into Magic Johnson, she started doing some really weird stuff. She would come into the living room while I was watching TV, put her arm around me, and have a miniature pep rally. She'd say, "We're gonna do it. It's just an adjustment we have to make. It's you and me, kid." I kept thinking that at any minute a whole army of cheerleaders would jump out from behind the sofa and start bouncing up and down with pom-poms. "Jack and Mom, Jack and Mom, they're our gang. If they can't do it, neither can Dad."

And then, while I'm right in the middle of feeling totally terrible for my mother and thinking that my dad's an absolute jerk for leaving without putting the storm windows up, she started going out on dates. It was only a couple of months after my dad packed. His gardening shoes were still out on the back porch like he'd be back in a minute or two. The goddamned lamp on my desk still had the same bulb in it. She started inviting total Webtones over for dinner and made me run around all afternoon cleaning house.

Even worse, and more unbelievable, I did everything she told me. It was the only time in my entire life that I had to vacuum the sofa and use fifty stain removers to try and get the grape Kool-Aid out of the front-hall carpet.

"We're going to have company for dinner," she'd say, like Colonel Sanders himself was gracing us with his presence. "We're having company," she'd say, like I was supposed to be happy about the whole thing. "I hope you'll join us."

"Boring," I'd say.

"Well, we'd love to have you at the table."

"I've got things to do besides eating with you and whoever," I finally yelled after three hundred dinners.

"Henry's his name."

"Whatever. I'm sure next week it'll be someone else. The turnover here is higher than in Congress."

"I don't like it when you talk to me like that. I don't like it one bit."

"Well, I don't like having dinner with John, Paul, George, and Ringo every night."

"Don't try and tell me how to live!" she screamed back.

And just like I thought maybe cheerleaders would pop out during her pep rallies, I kept hoping that during the fights a referee would blow the whistle and order her back to her corner.

Eventually, after a million dinners and three-quarters of a

million fights, I stopped answering her and she started eating out a lot. I felt guilty. First I'd driven my dad out of the house, and then I made my mom into some strange, hysterical restaurant critic. Maybe not literally, but I felt like it, and that's what counts. Personally, I turned into one of those creepy kids who's always at someone else's house, especially around dinnertime. I don't know why, but macaroni and cheese with wimpy broccoli on the side beat sitting alone in a booth at McDonald's.

Two years and a million months into this weirdness, and well past my fourteenth birthday, my mother decided that my father was allowed to take me out to dinner once a week. Before that he was actually allowed to see me every now and then for big events like my birthday, his birthday, George Washington's birthday, and all that, but it was always incredibly awkward.

The new once-a-week thing turned into a Julia Child class in important eating. Every Wednesday night, he'd take me to some totally fancy and inappropriate restaurant, as though spending fifty dollars on some thick slice of dead cow dunked in sauce was going to prove that he still loved me.

While we were eating, he'd ask forty questions about my mother: Was she happy, working hard, turning down the heat at night, and on and on until I wondered why the hell he didn't just ask her himself. Eventually, he cooled the questions about whether I thought my mom was depressed and was the hot-water heater leaking and started talking about things like love.

"What do you think about love?" he asked me in the middle of a restaurant, right while the waiter was standing there to see if everything was okay.

The waiter smiled to himself and walked away.

"I dunno." What the hell kind of question is that?

"Do you know what it means?" he asked.

I wasn't even going to answer, but then I saw him looking at me the way parents sometimes do.

"Yeah, sure," I said.

"Tell me what love is," he said.

I shook my head. There are certain games a person knows better than to play. "It's not something I can talk about," I said.

My dad pushed his plate away. "Well," he said. "There are lots of different kinds of love. People love doing things like going out to dinner and to the movies. Your mother loves reading the paper and smoking, and you love basketball."

Maybe my father was spending too much time alone and it was starting to affect him in a strange way. "Are you sure you're okay?"

"You can also love other people—your parents, your friends, your husband or wife."

"I'm not brain-damaged," I said. "At least, not severely."

"All kinds of people. It's not something you can control, although you can try. It just happens." He paused. "Jack, love doesn't have limits."

He said that and then sat there staring at me for a while.

"I'll be sure to remember that," I said, looking around for the waiter so I could order another Coke.

◇   ◇   ◇

As my mother liked to say, I adjusted. For what it's worth. I didn't exactly *love* to see my father pull up in the old blue Volvo and stand in the middle of the street, blowing the horn, waiting for me to come running out. It was like every time he picked me up, he announced to the whole world, or at least to everyone on our street, that he didn't have anything to do with our house, our family, or especially my mother anymore. It made me nauseous. He wouldn't even pull into the driveway when it was pouring rain. We were officially divorced.

I grew up. I made the AA basketball team and I didn't hate my mom's latest boyfriend, Michael Moore. He was a carpenter she'd originally hired to replace all the rotted-out windowsills, who finally moved in and kind of replaced my dad, at least in the home-repair category.

Michael wasn't anything like the other guys who'd been coming over for dinner in suits and ties, faking they were my best buddy. Michael looked more like a telephone pole with a beard than some used-car salesman trapped in a modern variation of a straitjacket. He always wore incredibly old wide-wale corduroys that hung off his body like there were no bones inside. He also had a real slow way of talking, which was okay unless you were in a hurry, and then you could rupture something before he got his thoughts out.

So there I was—all adjusted, fourteen and three-quarter years old, on the b-ball team, finally growing more hair on my legs than my mother—sitting on the front step waiting for my dad to collect me for the traditional divorced-father-divorced-kid Sunday adventure that meant having a whole lifetime squeezed into eight hours. He pulled up, and I got in.

We drove to dinky lake watchmayoyo about two miles from the house. The whole way there he kept asking me about Michael, who'd pretty much become full-time.

"He's a builder, right?"

"A carpenter."

"Oh, well, he's nice to your mother, right?"

"Guess so."

"You like him?"

"He's okay," I said.

I remember wishing he'd drop the subject. I felt like a spy, or an informer, or a regular lousy person, talking about people when I should have just kept quiet.

We rented a rowboat, and my dad spent about ten minutes making sure there were enough life preservers for a hundred people.

He'd spent my whole life playing safety officer. You know, putting little plugs into the electrical outlets so I couldn't stick a fork in. My dad had a serious thing, like a phobia, that I'd do something stupid like fall out a window or slip and drown in the bathtub. He told me not to play near the curb in a way that sounded like he knew for a fact a trash truck was purposely going to run me over or something.

The truly bizarre part of it was that I'm not at all accident-prone. He is. All the same, he was always there, ready to dial 911.

When he finished counting the life preservers and checking the boat for leaks, he let me get in and then rowed us out to the middle of the lake.

As soon as we were out there in the middle of nothing, he started getting the look fathers get when they're about to say something they know is gonna make you lose your lunch. It's a classic thing. Their eyebrows bunch together, and then they lean forward and say something like, Son, we need to talk. Then they pause for about half an hour and you practically have a heart attack while you're waiting. Finally, they say something like, Your grandmother's very ill, which usually means she's already dead but they're saving that for tomorrow.

This time it was even worse because he wasn't talking about someone being sick or anything like that. He was trying to tell me something about himself. He stopped rowing.

"Jack," he said. "I need to talk to you."

I nodded.

"I've been spending a lot of time trying to figure things out."

His voice was cracking all over the place.

"It's not an excuse. And I don't know if you're going to understand what I have to tell you."

He reached out and grabbed my arm. I pulled away. It wasn't as if I meant to; it just happened, like I was on autopilot or something.

"Jack, what I'm trying to say is that all these years, even back before you were born, I've been running away from myself, and a person can't do that forever. It begins to catch up."

I sat there staring down at the broken oarlocks, trying to figure out what the hell he was talking about. The green paint on the boat was chipping and a sort of punk fluorescent orange poked through.

"What?" I said.

"I realized . . ." He paused. "I'd be happier if I didn't live with your mother."

"I thought that was awhile ago."

He wasn't listening.

"I love her," he said. "I always will. But I'm happy now, living with another man."

I must have given him a pretty funny look at that point,

but I don't think I realized what he was saying.

"Jack, I've fallen in love with another man."

He stopped for a second and drew in his breath.

"You know Bob?" he asked.

Bob was his old friend, a guy he'd just rented an apartment with.

"Bob, the guy we went on that trip with, the guy who's your roommate now?"

He gave me a funny look, a very funny look. It didn't make sense.

"Bob and I, we sleep together."

I cut him off. "What are you talking about?"

"We're lovers." He blurted it out, an explosion like a firecracker.

I looked out at the water. Dragonflies were hovering over the scum. I wanted to get up, to run, but thanks to my dad, we were in the middle of a goddamned lake. I thought I was going to throw up. I could taste it in the back of my mouth.

"I'm sick," I said.

My father leaned into the oars and rowed to the dock. I jumped out and started running. After about a quarter mile, I slowed down to a walk. I'm not a goddamned marathon runner.

My dad was in the car behind me, but I didn't turn around. He passed me and stopped.

"Get in, I'll give you a ride."

"I'll walk," I said.

He took his foot off the brake and coasted next to me.

"Jack, I'm your father. I love you."

"Get away," I said.

"Don't act this way. Don't do this to me."

"Do what?" I yelled. "You're the one who did it."

I walked faster, but he kept the car at my side. From the corner of my eye I could see him steering with one hand and leaning out the window to talk to me.

"Jack, I told you. I didn't have to, but I thought you should know. It's okay. It doesn't have to change anything. You're my boy, my son."

I walked the whole way home with him trailing behind me like a lost dog. I went up the front steps into the house. My mom was sitting in the kitchen talking to her friend Elaine— Max's mom—on the phone.

"Jack?" she said when I slammed the door.

"Don't bother."

"They're back," she said to Elaine. "I'll call you later."

"Go ahead, talk to her now. Tell her the whole story. I'm sure you will, if you haven't already."

I ran up the steps to my room. From my window I could see my father parked in the middle of the street, hanging out the window of the goddamned car.

I stayed in my room all night, trying to figure out how my father could be queer. I mean, historically, queers are not fathers.

◇   ◇   ◇

When I walked into the kitchen the next morning, my mother didn't say anything. I didn't even get one of those sad-puppy-dog looks she used to give me all the time right after my dad left. She was standing at the stove, with a giant apron over her real-estate clothes, making whole wheat pancakes. My father always liked pancakes.

"Important to start right," he said practically every morning while he made breakfast. My mother never ate in the morning, so she never cooked either.

"You want it, you make it," was her motto.

"What's all the food?" Michael asked. He was wearing the old black sweat suit he called his meditation outfit.

"It's for Jack. He's a growing boy."

"A growing boy with a faggot father," I mumbled, but no one heard me, or more likely our senses were so stunned by my mother's culinary efforts that we couldn't hear anything.

Usually, my mother sat at the kitchen table with the morning paper spread out all over the place, a cup of coffee in one hand and her first cigarette in the other.

My father hated it when she smoked. "Do you have to do that first thing in the morning?" he would ask.

She never answered.

"In the kitchen, always in the kitchen. Everything in here smells like cigarettes. My goddamned toast tastes mentholated."

He used to go on for a couple of minutes, and my mom would totally ignore him until he sat down. Then she'd fold up the paper, put out her stub, and say, "Good morning."

Now, she was standing there, dressed in her work outfit, all ready to sell houses to happy families, coffee cup in one hand and a spatula in the other, her cigarette resting on the counter, burning a little trough in the Formica.

Michael poured orange juice for himself and me, picked up her stogie, took a drag—even though he claimed he never smoked—dunked the butt under the faucet, and threw it into the trash.

My mom put a giant stack of pancakes down in front of me. The sweet steam drifted up my nose, and for a minute I thought I might barf at the table.

"Go ahead, Jack, eat," my mom said.

She was smiling down at me in a fake motherly way that looked like it'd been clipped from the pages of *Family Circle*.

I didn't have the nerve to say anything, but whenever I eat heavy stuff like pancakes first thing in the morning, I'm totally nauseated for the next three weeks.

"Pass the syrup," Michael said.

I handed him the sticky bottle and watched as he poured gallons of one-hundred-percent-pure-Vermont cavities all over his plate.

My mother sat down and stared at me. She kept running her fingers through her hair like maybe she thought it was all going to fall out.

I ate in total silence, listening to Michael reading the paper out loud to himself.

"Anything on your mind?" my mom asked when I got up and put my plate in the sink.

"I'll miss the bus."

I ran upstairs to get my stuff, and when I came back she was standing at the door, half-blocking it, like she wasn't going to let me out.

"Thanks for breakfast," I said, slipping my knapsack over my shoulder, giving her a clue that it would be a good moment to move out of the way. "See ya," I said, and she was still standing there. "Good-bye," I said, moving her out of my way.

"You sound like a one-night stand, signing off," she said, putting a hand on each side of my head, covering my ears. "We'll talk later."

Her voice sounded like it was coming across a desert, or through a windstorm.

I could see Michael in the kitchen, his hands behind his

head, leaning back against the wall, waiting for my mom.

She kissed my forehead. "I love you," she said.

I ran out the door.

"And your father loves you, too."

At school, I had one of those days where no matter what anyone asked me, I couldn't come up with the right answer. Twice, Mr. Shapiro, my English teacher, asked if I felt all right. He said I looked "peak-ed." During lunch, I ate everything on my tray, even the stuff I didn't recognize. But the trouble didn't officially start until gym class.

I started really losing it when George Simpson took his gym suit out of his locker and shut himself into one of the bathroom stalls to change. I knew what would happen next only because it happened every day. I closed my eyes for a minute, thinking it might somehow stop everything. I closed my eyes and saw my dad sitting in the damn rowboat, confessing. Andrew Weilly, who used to be one of my friends, went over to the stall and started banging on the door.

"Come on, faggot, open up."

His voice came down hard on the word *faggot,* and my skin felt like it was shrinking while I was still wearing it.

"How come you don't change with us, little queer."

"Look," Peter Mathas said in a very excited way that, if you thought about it for a minute, sounded incredibly queer. "The homo's legs are prettier than my sister's."

I could see George moving around in the stall trying to make his legs invisible.

"Get outa there," I yelled, banging my fists on the metal stall door in a completely unintentional imitation of Robert DeNiro or someone.

Everyone seemed surprised; not on account of the New York accent—they didn't even know what one was. Their shock came from the fact that I'd never participated in the tormenting of George. In fact, usually I was the one who tried to get them to stop.

"Get the fuck outa there," I yelled.

I tried to rip the door off its hinges. At that moment I hated George more than anyone in the world. Even if he wasn't queer, I despised him for being a suspect. Almost everyone in the locker room had changed and gone outside. George finally unlocked the stall. I punched him hard in the stomach and on the back as he ran past me and up the stairs.

"I hate faggots," I yelled. "I swear I do."

Andrew slammed his locker shut and walked out with another guy. I spent the first half of the period trying to rip George's locker out of the wall and the second half sitting on the cold blue-and-white tile, my back pressed against my locker, crying like an idiot.

◇   ◇   ◇

"We're gonna talk," my mother said when she came home. She handed me a large white pizza box and went upstairs to ditch her real-estate clothes.

She was always afraid to be in the kitchen in her polyester stuff on account of how if it catches fire, it doesn't just burn, it melts, right into your skin.

"We're gonna eat and we're gonna talk," she said when she sat down, normalized with a cigarette, blue jeans, and one of her six Mickey Mouse sweatshirts.

She seemed determined. It was lucky she brought the pizza because I didn't know what the hell to say.

"Your father spoke to you yesterday."

I nodded and almost choked on a piece of pepperoni.

"And what did he say?"

I couldn't answer. I wouldn't answer. I didn't want to talk about it. It was bad enough he'd told me. I figured now it was my job to forget it, to pretend it didn't happen, it wasn't true.

"He told you that he loves you? And he told you that he lives with a man?"

I went to the sink and got a glass of water.

"He told you he sleeps with Bob. They're lovers. Do you know what that means?"

I ran the water hard so I didn't have to hear the last part, even though I knew what she was saying.

"Is there anything you want to discuss about it? Do you have any questions?"

I drank the whole glass of water and then another whole glass before I sat down.

"Why is he doing this?"

She lit a cigarette even though there was already one burning in the ashtray right in front of her. She lit a cigarette and didn't answer me.

"How long has it been going on? When did you find out?"

"I don't remember exactly," she said.

"Did he just come right out and tell you?"

"Why is it so important to know how and when?"

"Before he moved out?" I asked.

I felt like Mike Wallace on "60 Minutes." I didn't feel like a good guy, but there was stuff I needed to know—facts.

"When he moved into the other room? Tell me when."

She looked down at the floor, swept some dust around with her foot, and took a deep drag from her cigarette.

"I guess so," she said.

I figured. I figured it was then, the night with the lamp.

"Remember how your father was always going through a

phase—gardening, music, car repair? It was always something. He even went to New York once for a Miles Davis collector convention."

I didn't care about Miles Davis. "Would you still have gotten divorced if he hadn't told you?"

"It doesn't work that way," she said. "Your father left because we couldn't live together anymore. We used to argue. The house is quieter now, isn't it?"

Our house was like a morgue. I heard Michael drive up, and a few minutes later his key turned in the front door.

"I'm home," Michael said, like it wasn't obvious. No, Michael, you're not home, it's not you, it's just your aura, an aura with a key.

"In here," my mother said.

"Am I interrupting?"

From the look Michael gave my mother, I could tell he knew what we were talking about and that it was probably planned for him to come home late.

"There's still pizza," she said. "Microwave it."

Michael stuffed three pieces into the toaster oven. He was afraid of the microwave, but wouldn't admit it.

"I promised I'd call Elaine," she said, leaving the table, stubbing out her cigarette in the empty pizza box.

Michael sat there, staring at me, waiting for his slices to get hot. He didn't say anything, just sat there, rubbing his beard and watching.

I mean, Michael's a great guy and all. He's really into this Zen stuff, which is a philosophy that teaches you to be totally calm, no matter what. Michael always says that you have to learn to go with things the way they are, or something like that.

"Does she ever talk to you about my father?" I asked when

he'd stopped looking at me long enough to get his pizza out of the oven.

"Sometimes."

Sometimes Michael can be kind of spare with words, like sometimes he doesn't say anything. I looked at him, waiting for him to add to what he'd said.

"Well?" I said.

Michael put his pizza on the table and got a beer.

"Well," he said. "Your mom has attitudes about things. She wants people to be a certain way, the same way she is. But it doesn't always go like that."

"What about my father?"

"He's not her favorite character."

We didn't say anything for a while. I could hear my mother up in her room, talking to Mrs. Burka on the phone. She sounded annoyed.

All of the sudden, I started wishing I was a little kid again, with a mom, a dad, no complications.

"It'll be all right," Michael said.

"Did you ever meet him?"

"Once, by accident."

"Well, my dad's queer, you know."

"I know," Michael said.

"Great, how come no one ever told me? The whole damn world knows everything and somehow I got left out. How come things just happen around here? How come no one's in control?" I stopped for a second. "He borrowed my lamp. He moved out, and no one said a word, not one iddly-piddly little word. I'm not allowed to see him, and then I am allowed to see him, and then he rows me out to some damn lake and tells me he's queer."

"They thought they were protecting you. Your mom felt like she had to take care of you, Jack. You were still a kid when he left."

I wasn't listening. "How could he be a homo? I'm his son, right, or is there something else no one told me?"

Michael shook his head.

"It makes me sick, seriously. My father's a fucking faggot."

I didn't talk for a while. I didn't hear my mother talking on the phone anymore. She was probably lurking around the corner, listening or watching or something, I didn't care.

"Jack, because your father is gay is no reason for you to be dramatic. It doesn't mean anything."

Michael got another beer. I hated him for calling me dramatic. It implied that I was faking, that I shouldn't be taken seriously, that I was hysterical. I *hated* the word *dramatic;* it was like some Shakespearean death scene.

"Are you an alcoholic?" I asked.

He shook his head.

"Know any queers?"

"A few. If you stopped calling them queer, it would probably help."

"Help who? They're queer. I mean, it's not the normal thing."

"Who's to say what's normal?"

Old Mr. Zen was sitting there treating me like I was one of him, one of those philosophical wizards who have their lives all laid out in a nice crooked line in front of them. But, I was still a kid. The only things I saw laid out in a line were the foul line, the baseline, and the shortest route to first base.

"You think your dad's all right, don't you?" he asked.

I didn't answer; it was pointless.

"You guys go to the movies, play ball, you talk to him?"

"Before," I said.

"Not before," Michael insisted. "He's the same person. He didn't have to tell you. Whatever he said out on the lake didn't really have anything to do with you. He was talking about himself. One day you're going to have to make the same choices."

"I'm certainly not going to be queer," I said.

I didn't say anything else. If I was queer, I'd kill myself. I don't know why, but I swear I would. I sat at the table half-hoping a bolt of lightning or something would crash through the window and stab me in the chest, just so I wouldn't have to deal with this anymore.

"You're worrying too much," Michael said.

"No, I'm just being dramatic," I said in a perfect imitation of his voice.

He looked hurt. He picked up the pizza box and stuffed it in the trash.

"Your night for garbage," he said.

Michael ran his hand through his hair. It was something he did a lot, like it cleared his head or something.

"Your dad's a nice guy. He loves you. Like him for what he is, not what he isn't."

Then Mr. Zen took a third bottle of beer out of the fridge and went upstairs.

◇   ◇   ◇

Right after my dad's boating lesson, I started going out with Ann McCormick. Not really going out, like on dates or anything, but all of a sudden I was holding her hand all over the place. The thing I have to admit is that the major reason I made her walk all over the school holding my hand was so no would would think I was a homo, or anything anywhere near it. We didn't really have much to say to each other, but she had nice hands, soft and not a bit clammy.

My mother knew, but didn't mention it until one night when Ann came over for dinner.

"What do you think?" I asked my mom.

"Of what?"

"You know, Ann?"

I was in the kitchen helping her do the dishes. Ann was sitting in the living room talking to Michael.

"She seems nice," my mother said. "What do you think?"

"I dunno," I mumbled.

I washed a few more dishes.

"She's got braces."

"I noticed that," my mother said.

"Food gets stuck in them."

"Well, that's the way things go. She won't always have braces."

"At least till the end of eleventh grade. The orthodontist told her."

"That's not forever."

"I know," I said. "But, she's kind of stupid—"

My mother cut me off. "Shhh. You're not being nice and you're talking too loud."

"Yeah, well, she's not the greatest, okay."

I threw my towel down on the counter.

"I hate to tell you, Jack, but she probably feels the same way about you."

"I'm not sure she feels anything," I said, thinking of the time I tried to tell her about my family.

"Then stop going around with her."

"No."

"Why not, if you don't like her?"

"All the kids know I'm going out with a girl."

"What?"

Sometimes mothers can be a real pain; they always want to know why and what for.

"It looks good," I said, and started to walk out of the kitchen.

"I have never . . ." She started to say something, but couldn't finish. "I want to talk to you later," she said. "After your company's gone."

I went back into the living room and sat down on the sofa next to Ann. She and Michael were talking about some book by a Japanese guy I never heard of. I could tell Ann was trying to impress Michael by going on and on about how wonderful this guy was, and wasn't his philosophy what life is really all about. Michael was sitting in our big overstuffed chair, the one that my dad always used to sit in, the one my parents bought together at some auction when I was about two, and I kind of halfway remember it. He was smiling and nodding at Ann, acting like she was incredibly intelligent. I could tell that as soon as she left, Michael would pull me aside and say something like, "People who really know what they're talking about don't have to talk at all."

Ann went on forever, and when she finally stopped for air, I jumped up.

"Come on. I'll walk you home," I said. "I'm sure you have homework or something to do tonight."

I wanted to say, like getting the food out of your braces, but I didn't.

She said good-bye and thanked my mother too much for dinner.

Ann lived about three blocks away. It didn't take me very

long to walk her home, especially because I made her cut through the Millers' backyard even though she didn't want to.

"It's dark," she kept saying.

"It gets that way at night," I said.

"We can't go here—it's private property."

"If you don't keep announcing it, they'll never notice."

"The grass is all wet."

I grabbed her arm and practically pulled her home. She didn't say anything else. I think she liked me holding her hand, even though I was almost ripping it off. She kept trying to rest her head on my shoulder as we walked, but it didn't work well; she was maybe three inches taller and I was walking pretty fast on account of being in a rotten mood. When we got to her house, I could see her dad sitting in the living room watching TV, and her mother talking on the phone.

"Bye," I said, and I jumped off the porch and ran home.

"Jack," my mother said when I walked in the front door. "Come in here."

She was sitting at the kitchen table talking to Michael, who was finishing the bottle of wine they'd opened at dinner.

"I'm not sleeping with her if that's what you're worried about. In fact, I'm not even planning on it."

I looked at Michael. He smiled even though he obviously knew I was getting myself in trouble. It was a thing between boys. He knew I had to do it anyway.

"It's very nice for you to have a girlfriend," my mom said. "You should have girlfriends *and* boyfriends."

I wanted to start laughing because at that moment the whole thing seemed pretty funny.

"You don't particularly like her, do you?"

I didn't know what to say; it wasn't really funny.

"She's got nice hands. They're soft and not at all clammy."

"It's because of your father," she said. "You should know that."

I didn't like the way it sounded. It sounded like there was no way I'd have a girlfriend if my dad wasn't gay. But in some crazy way I knew it was true. I had no business doing anything with girls.

"So," I said, like I could use one word, spoken in the right tone, to defend myself.

"Jack," she said. "It would be very wrong of you to go out with Ann just because you have something to prove to yourself. Very wrong."

Her voice sounded sharper than a Swiss army knife.

"It's a horrible, rotten thing to do to someone, to use them to make you feel better about yourself. Believe me, I know."

As soon as she finished, she jumped up from the table, ran upstairs, and slammed the bedroom door.

I shrugged at Michael and looked down at the floor. The white tiles had gone gray, and there was a heavy black line of dirt where the grout used to be. My father was a shithead and so was I. Michael tilted the bottle of wine up and poured the last few drops down his throat.

"Well," I finally said.

"She does have a point."

"I'm not really even going out with her."

"Jack," he said, and then stopped.

Michael threw the empty wine bottle across the room and into the trash. What normal adult throws big glass bottles across a room? It didn't even break.

"It reminds her of your father. He used your mother to protect himself."

Mr. Zen strikes again. Michael went downstairs to check the hot-water heater and I went out front and practiced hook shots until my mother banged on the window and said I was giving her a headache.

After that, I kept my hands to myself. I told Ann that it was nothing personal but I wasn't ready to be involved—in anything, including my own life.

◇ ◇ ◇

The Tuesday after he confessed, my dad called to make sure I was keeping our usual Wednesday dinner appointment. I refused to talk to him, so he asked Michael to put my mom on the phone. Michael opened the front door and yelled out to her. She was in the yard playing late-night gardener, planting flowers even though it was pitch-dark. She came inside, turned off the flashlight, took the receiver and tucked it under her ear.

"It's not easy," she said.

No hello, no how are you.

"It's all very simple for you, like redecorating, but things aren't that way for all of us." She paused.

It was obvious that what she was saying had been building up in her for a while. I couldn't help but think that the decorating line was a super cut-down, a bad fag joke, even though I'm sure she didn't realize it.

"Okay, so maybe I have no idea of what's simple for you. I don't care."

She stopped again, this time holding the receiver away from her ear. I could hear my father yelling. It reminded me of the phone calls when he first moved out.

"All I'm trying to say," she said, "is that it's hard for him to comprehend. Hell, it's still hard for me. He's just trying to grow up and, if you can remember, that's bad enough without all the shit you just dumped on him."

She stopped talking. Michael was standing next to her, pawing at the old Kool-Aid stain on the carpet with his sock.

"If he doesn't want to talk to you, you can't force him. He's angry with you, damn it. You deserted him."

She handed the phone to Michael, turned on her flashlight, and went back into the yard.

"I think she's upset," Michael said to my dad. "You should know she's being wonderful about the whole situation, talking to Jack, everything."

What was Michael, a social worker, an eyewitness news reporter, an idiot?

I watched Michael's head nod up and down while my dad talked.

"Give a call back later in the week."

Michael hung up and my mother came back into the house.

"How can you be so nice," she screamed. "I don't want you to be so nice. And don't ever tell him I'm upset again."

She shook her flashlight in his face. The beam swept back and forth across his eyes, nose, and mouth. She went out the door and two seconds later came in again.

"It's not fair. He spills his guts to Jack and leaves me to clean up the mess. It's typical. I bet they're all like that. They never work things out, never stay to the finish, just fight, pack, and leave."

Michael put his hands on her shoulders.

"Don't touch me."

She pushed him away with the flashlight and went back out into the yard. Michael stood in the door, watching her. Eventually, he went into the kitchen to start dinner, and I went out to talk to her.

"Mom?" I said.

She sat on the ground, the flashlight tucked under her chin, digging holes with an oversize kitchen spoon.

"If you want to talk, you have to dig," she said, handing me a small shovel.

"Are you mad at me because of this stuff with Dad?"

"God, no."

A hunk of dirt flipped out of her spoon and grazed the side of my face.

"Sorry," she said.

"You're acting weird."

"What are you talking about?"

She dropped a half-wilted geranium into a hole and covered the roots with dirt.

"Breakfast. You never used to make breakfast." I paused. "I get nauseous when I eat in the morning."

"You're thin. I wanted to make sure you're getting enough to eat."

The flashlight slipped out from under her chin and fell onto the grass. The beam lit up the lawn like it was time for "Monday Night Football."

"I go out in a damn rowboat and Dad tells me he's a homo. I just want to know what's going on."

"Nothing. Nothing is going on. You know it all now."

"Why don't you act regular? Why are you guys telling me this now?"

"We thought you could handle it. We thought you were grown-up enough."

I jabbed my shovel into the dirt. My mom handed me the flashlight. I tucked it under my chin so it pointed down to where I'd been digging. I saw a worm I'd just cut in half with the shovel, trying to crawl away. It was slightly crushed at both ends.

"Act regular," she said, standing up. "I can't." She wiped

the dirt off the knees of her pants. "It's hard for me, too, Jack. He's your father, but he used to be my husband, and that didn't work. Don't you think sometimes maybe I wonder why?"

"It's Dad's fault. He's the queer."

"Fault. Maybe it was me, Jack. Maybe I did something wrong. Maybe I wasn't a good enough wife, a good enough mother. I smoke too much. I never clean the house. I hate doing laundry. I don't make breakfast. I read the paper all morning. Maybe it was me."

"You're a good mother," I said, hugging her. "Don't ever think you aren't. It's Dad. I hate him. I swear, I hate him."

She touched the side of my face with her dirty hand. "I was so horrible, I'm sorry," she said, and then ran back into the house to make up with Michael, leaving me outside in the dark, with a flashlight under my chin, planting flowers.

◇   ◇   ◇

"You're so weird," Max Burka, my best friend, said during lunch.

"Thank you for announcing it. I'm glad the whole world knows. Truly, I'm thrilled."

"What is this, anyway?" he said, grabbing the front of my much-too-big flannel shirt and pulling it toward him. "A nightgown?"

"It was my father's," I said, pulling away, thinking that if the shirt ripped I'd have cause to kill.

"Oh, so it's like holy," Max said.

I hated my dad, but I loved him also, which made it worse. My life, even just being friends with stupid Max, was too complicated.

"You gonna eat this stuff?"

Max poked his finger around in my mixed vegetables. I shook my head.

"I had a big breakfast," I said.

Max mushed the veggies into what the cafeteria called mashed potatoes—I'm positive it really was papier-maché—and then forked the whole mess into his mouth.

"You're so gross," I said as I watched him eat.

He nodded in agreement. I started playing with the saltshaker.

"What do you think of queers?"

Max got up and moved down a seat. He thought it was funny.

"What do you mean?"

He stuffed something into his mouth that was supposed to be apple cobbler but looked more like an environmental sculpture.

"Nothing, just what do you think?"

"I dunno," he said, pushing my empty tray away and wiping his hands on his thighs.

Max had class, that was for sure.

"I guess it's a disease," he said. "Sickness, same as the guys who chop up their families and stick the pieces under the house."

"You're sick," I mumbled.

"I once heard my dad telling someone about a guy who was married, had a kid and everything, and then all of a sudden, like out of the blue, decided he was queer."

I shriveled up inside my father's shirt. My father and Max's father were good friends, or used to be good friends. I was glad I hadn't eaten lunch, because if I had, it would have been all over the place.

"What'd he say?" I looked down at the floor and tried to

be calm, hoping my voice didn't give me away.

"That's all. My mother told him it was nothing to talk about, so he shut up."

Ralph Ryan walked by, and Max stuck his foot out into the aisle and tripped him.

"Know any queers?" Max asked.

"How come?" Ralph asked.

Ralph had ice cream on his nose and down the front of his shirt.

"Taking a survey," Max said.

"Russ Miller's brother's queer," Ralph said.

"Did you eat the whole cone?" Max asked.

I was surprised he didn't ask if he could lick the drips off Ralph's shirt. Even though he ate like a pig, Max only weighed about one-fifteen, ten pounds more than I did.

"How do you know he's a fag?"

"Russ's father came home early from work once and caught him running around in a dress, high heels and all. Can you believe, a fucking dress?"

"No kidding," Max said. "I bet all faggots wear dresses around the house."

I clubbed him across the head. It was a habit. I always hit him when he said stupid things. It was surprising that he wasn't black-and-blue all over.

"What are you," I said to Max. "*Encyclopaedia Britannica* or something? You don't know what you're saying and already you're talking."

"They kicked him out," Ralph said. "He went to New York or somewhere and he writes Russ these letters all the time, but his parents won't let him read them. They're afraid he'll get AIDS from them or something."

"Jeez," Max said. And then he looked at me real seriously. He looked me straight in the eye and, like he meant it, he said, "You don't have AIDS, do you Jack?" I nearly died, and while I was dying Max collapsed onto the cafeteria floor, laughing his head off. "It was a joke. You're a virgin, don't you get it," he said, laughing absolutely hysterically. "Virgins can't get AIDS."

"You're an idiot," I said, and I walked away with my legs still shaking.

"Jack," Max whined. "Where are you going?"

"Library. See you later."

"Wait for me," he said.

I stacked my tray and walked through the double doors, alone.

◇   ◇   ◇

The librarian looked at me funny when I asked her for books on homosexuality.

"It's for a science project," I said.

"Use the card catalog," she said. There were no books listed. I mean, they spend a hundred years teaching you how to look stuff up in the infamous card catalog, but there's never anything you actually need in it.

Basically, I guess junior-high libraries aren't known for their broad range of reading materials. They've got two sets of the *World Book*, a dictionary, eighteen pamphlets on venereal disease and safe sex, three hundred S. E. Hinton paperbacks, and a copy of last month's *National Geographic*, with the picture ripped out by some pervert.

While I was checking the magazine file, I noticed George Simpson curled up in the window reading. I thought about going over and saying hi or something, but as soon as he saw me, he grabbed his books and literally ran out of the library.

In the magazine file there were a couple of articles on homosexuality mixed in with the rest of the stuff. I'm convinced that if the librarian knew they were there, she would have thrown them out. One article said that one in ten people is homosexual and that there seem to be more now than ever before—probably because everyone's taking their kids out in rowboats and confessing. The articles also said that AIDS isn't just going to kill gay men and drug addicts, but everyone, so the government better spend more time trying to figure out how to cure it, and that gay rights is the biggest political issue since the civil-rights movement. I rolled up the articles and stuffed them into my pocket.

◇　　　　　◇　　　　　◇

My dad called twenty times a day trying to get me to let him be my father again. I refused to talk to him. Finally my mother screamed at me.

"You're being incredibly obnoxious. He's your father," she said, jamming the phone into my hand.

"He's gay," I whispered to my mother, and she faked looking surprised. "Hi, Dad," I said.

"I want to see you," my father said. "We don't have to go anywhere, we could just talk."

The last thing I wanted to do was talk. But, to make him feel better, I agreed to go to a movie.

"Now," he said.

I felt like I didn't have a choice. He picked me up a half hour later. On the way to the movie theater, I kept looking at him, analyzing him to see if there was anything that looked particularly queer.

To me, he looked like a deranged Robert Redford. He had blond hair that looked fake only because it was so yellow, and blue eyes. In the right light, one eye looked bright green, like a coyote's.

As far as I could tell, he was the same guy who stole the lamp all those years ago. He still drove like a madman, staying in one gear until the engine nearly blew and then, at the very last minute, shifting, and practically throwing whoever was riding with him through the windshield.

The movie was by this guy who's one of my all-time heroes. It would have been great except for the nervous breakdown I was having on account of being out with my *gay* dad. The whole time I should have been watching the film, I sat there remembering how my parents always used to take me to the movies with them when I was little. It was cheaper than getting a baby-sitter. Halfway through, I'd usually curl up in my seat and fall asleep. Later, in the car, my mom would start singing some French song they supposedly heard six billion years ago on their honeymoon. Then, while my dad was driving along, they'd start kissing each other and laughing and I'd be in the backseat screaming because my dad wasn't watching the road and we kept going off onto the gravel.

"Not a romantic," my dad would say, reaching into the back and patting me on the head to get me to shut up. My mother would laugh even harder and start singing the stupid song again.

So anyway, I sat there in the movies with my dad, being a nervous wreck, remembering him making out with my mom, and wondering if he did stuff like that with Bob and exactly how it worked. I kept trying to pay attention to the movie, but it was no use.

I got up about forty times. Once for popcorn, then for a

Coke because I was choking to death on the popcorn. And then I had to get napkins because my hands were all greasy from the popcorn.

About fifteen minutes before the end, my dad leaned over and whispered in my ear. "Everything all right?"

"Yeah," I said, even though I wanted to say no.

I wanted to tell him that the chair was uncomfortable, that I definitely had gum stuck to the bottom of my shoe, and that I hated him. Instead, I sat there, waiting for the movie to end, watching the backs of people's heads, counting empty chairs and red exit signs.

"I don't have time to stop for dinner," my dad said on the way home. "One of our clients died and we need to go over some things with his family. Is that okay?"

"Sure," I said.

My dad was an accountant with a law firm. The facts-and-figures man. He asked me again if it was all right that he wasn't taking me to dinner. I kept getting the feeling that he expected me to yell, to tell him that the dead guy could take a walk and that he had to take me to dinner. He pulled up in front of the house and started apologizing all over again.

As a sick kind of personal joke, I thought of telling him that if he just drove the damn car into the driveway instead of hovering in the street like a spaceship, I'd forgive him.

He kind of grabbed me by the back of the neck and said, "I'm glad we're together."

And for a while he sat there, holding my neck like I was a baby and couldn't do it myself.

"Yeah, Dad, it was fun."

We were quiet and I could hear funny rumbling noises in the engine.

"Car's making a noise," I said.

"Bob and I are dropping it off at the shop tomorrow morning."

The way he said "Bob and I" sounded just like how he used to say "your mother and I," and I started hearing "Bob and I" rhyming with "your mom and I" in my head. I opened the door and got out.

"We'll have dinner during the week?"

"Sure," I said.

"You're home early," my mom said when I walked in.

She was sitting on the sofa with some guy I'd never seen before. I could tell he worked in her office because of the green polyester jacket he was wearing. Michael had gone away for a couple of days to "get some space," as he liked to say. Mr. Zen did stuff like that pretty often. It drove my mom crazy and she'd always invite some Webtone over. And even though I never said anything to Michael, I hated him for it.

"Jack, this is Bill Worth."

The guy looked at me like he was sizing up the competition for a wrestling match. He put his drink down on the coffee table, stood up, and mashed his clammy hand into mine.

"Did everything go all right?" my mom asked.

There was no way to answer with Webtone Bill standing there.

"Where'd he take you?"

"A movie."

"Any good?"

I felt like she was trying to prove I could talk so her friend wouldn't think I was retarded or something.

"I dunno."

"Well, it was good you went. Did you have dinner?"

"Dad had a meeting."

"Doesn't he like to feed you?"

She didn't normally talk like that. I wondered if she was doing it because of Bill or if it was another of her recent abnormal reactions.

"He could have at least bought you a hamburger. It figures."

"It's okay," I said. "I had popcorn and a Coke."

I went up the steps to my room.

"Bill and I are going out to dinner."

"You're welcome to join us," the Webtone said.

I knew he'd have a coronary if I even thought of going.

"I'll leave you some money in case you want McDonald's," my mom said.

I didn't answer. Something inside me said there was a better way out. I picked up my basketball and started bouncing it off the wall. It made little black marks every time it landed. I heard my mother and the polly-wanna-green-suit go out the front door.

After banging the basketball against the ceiling, the walls, and the floor for a half hour or so, I called Max.

"His father took him to a ball game, but they have to be back soon," Mrs. Burka said. "Dinner's almost ready."

When I was little, Mr. Burka and my dad used to take me and Max everywhere.

"I'm making sweet-and-sour chicken. Have you eaten?" she asked.

Usually, I ended up eating over at Max's house about twice a week. I guess you could say I was a regular.

"I had popcorn and Coke," I said.

"Come over," she said. "By the time you get here, Max

will be home and dinner will be on the table."

I always liked Mrs. Burka. She was the kind of person you didn't have to explain things to.

"Well, I dunno," I said.

"Sammy's already setting your place. Twenty minutes."

She hung up the phone. I went into the garden and picked some flowers for her. Sometimes I wished she was my mother. She always seemed to know exactly what she was doing.

"It's the guest for dinner," Sammy yelled when he opened the door and saw me standing there with flowers and my hair all combed.

"Come in," Mrs. Burka said from in the kitchen. "They just called a minute ago. A flat tire, but they're on the way."

She pulled the chicken out of the oven. It was a little burned across the top. I handed her the flowers. She smiled and thanked me. I don't know why, but I turned bright red. I looked at Mrs. Burka. I would have stared if only I could have figured out how to do it without getting caught. She had brown hair that always surprised me. Sometimes it was totally curly, as if she'd brushed it with an electric toothbrush. And other times it was totally straight and came out of her head like the branches of a Christmas tree. It was confusing as hell. I always wondered if it was something she did on purpose.

"You wanna see something," Sammy said, pulling me outside through the kitchen door. He pointed to what looked like a small stack of sticks. "It's my farm," he said.

"Twigs," I said.

"Look in the middle."

And sure enough, sort of propped up by all the sticks were a couple of skinny green plants.

"One's squashes and the other's lettuce," he said.

We sat down on Sammy's swing set. It groaned whenever I moved. I felt older than ever before.

"I remember when you were a baby," I said.

"I was smaller then," he said.

I really liked Sammy. If I ever had a kid, I'd want one like him.

"That's right," I said. "And you only had one eye."

"Not true."

He crossed his arms in front of him.

"I remember because I used to baby-sit you, and your mother was all upset because you only had one eye."

"Which one?"

"The right one," I said. "And where the other one was supposed to be, there was nothing. Your mom took you to all kinds of doctors, and finally one said that he'd seen lots of other kids with the same thing."

"What happened?"

"He told your mom to wait until you were two and that by then you'd have a second eye. So, we all waited, and about two weeks before your birthday you started to grow this other eye. It was kind of gross at first, but by your birthday it was a regular eye like anyone else's."

Sam didn't say anything. He ran back into the house and told the story to Mrs. Burka.

"You've always had two beautiful eyes," she said, hugging him.

"Told you it wasn't true," he said.

Mrs. B. kind of shook her head at me, but I could tell she thought it was funny.

"You shouldn't tease," she said.

"It was true," I said. "But it must have been some other little kid."

"What're you doing here?" Max said when he walked in.

"Having dinner, I guess."

"Who says?" Max demanded.

"I invited him," Mrs. Burka said.

Sometimes Max could be too much. I mean, right then and there, I kept looking at the door and gauging how long it would take me to run out of it.

"Max, go up and wash your face, it's filthy," she said.

"What about his face?"

Max pointed at Sammy, who was dipping his fingers into a bowl of applesauce.

"He has a lovely face," Mrs. Burka said.

Mr. B. sat down at the table, took a piece of chicken onto his plate, and started cutting it up into little pieces.

"Go wash," he said to Max. "Sit," he said to me. "How's your father?" he asked between bites.

"Okay," I said, looking down at the chicken.

I didn't want to get into a whole thing about my father on account of having a sinking feeling that he knew the whole story.

"I don't see him too much anymore," Mr. B. said.

Max sat down at the table, his face glowing with a scrubbed look. Mrs. Burka put a big spoonful of carrots onto my plate.

"You need a little color," she said.

"He lives downtown, close to the office," I said.

Guys like Mr. Burka could always relate to things that had to do with offices.

"A good guy to have around," Mr. Burka said.

He was talking to himself.

"Steady, fast on his feet, a nice hook shot. Too bad, huh?"

"Pardon me," I said, nearly choking on the chicken.

"Him and your mom. I shouldn't say anything, but I always

thought they should have stuck it out. We all have our problems."

He looked at Mrs. Burka.

"But time works them out."

"Would anyone like more chicken?" Mrs. Burka said, threatening to drop a drumstick onto my plate.

"Thanks, I'm full," I said.

She waved the drumstick toward Max. He burped loudly and shook his head. Sammy nodded, and she dropped it on his plate.

"I can always count on you," she said to him.

I helped Mrs. Burka clear the table while Max sat there watching and picking his teeth with the edge of his knife.

"I wanna show you something," he said when I finished.

I followed him downstairs.

"I'm restaging the Tet Offensive."

He pulled me toward a Ping-Pong table remade as Vietnam. There were little soldiers all over the place, a few tanks, and a jeep. Bomber jets hung from long strands of fishing line.

"I've just got to defoliate these trees," he said as he picked up a wonderfully thick green tree and ripped the greenness off until only the skeleton remained.

"It's a bitch that they don't sell these bald."

Max was getting weird. I couldn't help but wonder where it came from. Mrs. Burka was very normal and Sammy was great; that only left Mr. Burka.

"Okay. These guys sneak in and totally destroy this whole village, watch."

Max flipped a small switch and all of a sudden his toothpick-and-Popsicle-stick village exploded into flames.

"Max," Mrs. Burka yelled down the stairs. "I hope you're not playing with fire."

◇ 50 ◇

"It was just a little village," he said. "But I had to blow it."

"No fires," Mrs. Burka said.

"That's how they did it, ask my dad."

"Not in the basement," Mrs. Burka yelled. "Put it out."

"You wanna drop a bomb?" Max asked me.

His eyes were glowing like the war was a naked girl or something.

"No thanks."

He lifted his arm high above the smoldering village and dropped three firecrackers directly onto what had been a large hut. There was a short delay and then a quick bang, bang, bang, and pieces of the Popsicle-stick structure shattered, flew through the air, and landed all across the Ping-Pong table.

"Enemy supply station," Max said. "I knew it all along."

He dumped a cup of water onto the whole mess and watched as it fizzled and smoked. He poked at the ruins with a pencil.

"Never leave a campsite until you're sure the fire's completely out. Stirring the coals," he said, "is an old Boy Scout routine."

"You weren't a Scout," I said.

"No, but my dad was."

"That doesn't make you one."

◇   ◇   ◇

The phone rang six times before I realized my mother wasn't going to answer it. Getting out of bed, I stubbed my toes on the corner of the night table, and stumbled into the hall, positive that I'd amputated most of my foot.

"Hi Jack, how are you?" my dad said when I picked up the phone.

He sounded as though he'd been up for hours or at least had already eaten a big breakfast.

"Fine, same as yesterday."

I yawned and hooked my stubbed toes around the wrought-iron railing at the top of the stairs.

"How do you feel about bowling?" he asked.

I felt like I was being interviewed. "Big pins or little ones?"

I mean, I'm not exactly a bowling fan and as far as I knew neither was my father.

"There's someone I want you to meet. The daughter of a friend of mine."

"Is she a bowling fanatic?"

"Not that I know of. Her name's Margaret. Listen, you can bring Max if you want. It'll be fun. We'll get a hot dog, bowl a couple of rounds."

"Games, Dad, you bowl games and frames, not rounds."

"Whatever, I'll pick you up at six."

"What'd he want?" my mom asked from her door.

"Bowling tonight." I walked back toward my room.

"It's a school night."

"We're going at six."

"You should have asked."

"I'll call back and say I can't," I offered, more than willing. Bowling with the daughter of one of my dad's friends wasn't my idea of a great time.

"It doesn't matter," she said.

I shouldn't have bothered answering the phone. Some days are like that, I know, because someone once gave me a greeting card that warned me.

"Bowling?" Max said.

He was standing outside the science room, picking his nose.

"Since when do you bowl?"

"I don't. But I think my dad does."

"God," Max said, wiping his finger on his jeans. "Only totally queer people bowl."

Well, that explains it, I thought.

"What time?"

"Six," I said.

My dad pulled up in Old Blue at six-ten. I waited until he beeped before I let Max open the front door.

"You are so weird," Max said.

"Tell him you have to be home by eight," my mom said.

There was no way I was going to get into the car and say, Mom says I have to be home by eight, in front of some other kid, especially a girl I didn't even know. My dad was the only one in the car.

"Where's the girl?" Max asked.

"Meeting us there. Hi, Max," my dad said.

Max smiled and tried to be charming.

"You want the front seat?" I said to Max.

He nodded. It's really lucky I'm skinny; otherwise I wouldn't have fit into the back, on account of Max not being too knowledgeable about how the front seat tilts forward so someone can get in.

"Need any help?" Max asked when my legs got caught in the strap from the seat belt he wasn't too knowledgeable about wearing. The car made all these horrible sounds like it was falling apart, but then I realized it was just my dad putting it in gear.

"Margaret's dad works with Bob," my dad said.

"Great." I tried to sound enthusiastic.

"Who's Bob?" Max asked.

"My roommate," my dad said, and I caught him looking at me in the rearview mirror.

"Sevens please," I said to the fat, bald guy on the other side of the counter.

"Eleven and a half," my dad said.

"No half sizes," the guy said.

"Okay. Elevens."

"All out," the guy said.

"Twelves then," my dad said.

"Eight," Max said, and somehow I was angry that his feet were bigger than mine.

"So, where's the girl?"

My dad looked around. The bowling alley was practically empty.

"There." He pointed toward the very last lane.

Max and I followed him. There were two guys and a girl with long brown hair. One of the guys saw us coming and waved. He waved like a faggot, or like the queen of England. I wanted to go home. I wanted to cover Max's eyes. When we got up close, they stopped bowling and turned toward us. I looked down at my shoes.

"Frank, John, Margaret, this is Jack and Max," my dad said.

I was forced to look up. Margaret wasn't Margaret; she was Maggie Rogers, one of the most impossible girls in my grade. She hung out with the ultracool crowd, the kids who never, ever, talk to anyone but themselves. I shoved my hands into my pockets and turned green. The only thing missing was the yearbook photographer.

"You're Jack," she said. "Oh, wow."

"Sure am." I rocked back and forth on the heels of my bowling shoes and looked everywhere but at her.

"He's your dad." She pointed to my father, who was now, when I needed him, busy in some other conversation.

"Guess so," I said, still rocking.

"So, Mags," Max said. "You like to bowl a lot or what, like are you on a team?"

"It was Jack's father's idea," she said, as though she was sure that everyone in my family always had rotten ideas.

"Are you alone here or what?" Max asked.

I knew he was getting at the fact that you never saw the ultracools except in a crowd, pressed together like too many Siamese twins.

"I'm with my father," she said, pointing to the tall guy my dad was talking to. Her father was resting his arm on the other guy's shoulder. I hoped Max wasn't looking.

"Who's the other guy?" Max asked.

I wondered if it was close enough to eight that I could tell my dad I had to hurry home or my mom would be really, really angry and would never let me go out with him again.

"Jim or John, or something like that. He moved in last week. He'll be gone pretty quick. I can tell. He's gross."

"You guys run a boardinghouse or something?" Max said.

She looked at me. I shrugged. I didn't want to have anything to do with it, any of it.

Maggie was one of the nine million girls I was secretly in love with, but would never, ever have talked to under normal circumstances.

"He only speaks to me if my father is in the room. Otherwise he acts like I'm not there," she said.

"Are you guys gonna bowl, or is this just a sit-and-talk kind of thing?" Max said. "I mean, no problem, but if we're just gonna sit, I'll go get something to eat."

Max went over to check out the bowling balls and tripped on one of his shoelaces.

"Burpa," Maggie whispered. "That's what they call him.

He eats like a pig and burps in people's faces."

I nodded. "My best friend," I said. "From childhood."

"Take a couple of practice shots," my dad said. "And then we'll start.

I picked up the ball right near me and had to put it down immediately. I could feel a hernia coming on.

"Is there a problem?" Maggie's dad asked.

"It weighs more than I do."

"Pick another," he said.

I went over and tried them all until I finally found one that weighed nine pounds. It still felt too heavy, but the next-lighter one had Mickey Mouse stickers all over it and I just couldn't take it.

Maggie, Max, and I were on one team. My dad, Maggie's father, and John were on the other. I knew we were in trouble when the first three balls I bowled all went into the gutter. My dad, playing baby-style—rolling the ball with both hands, through his knees—got a strike on the first frame.

"Mags, it's up to you," Max said, handing Maggie the ball.

She held it in her right hand for a while, then switched to her left, walked up to the line, switched back to her right, and literally threw the ball down the alley. It bounced hard three times, echoing like gunshots, before settling into a roll and killing six pins.

"Way to go," Max said. "Make potholes, confuse the opponents."

He stood up to shake her hand. Maggie stuffed her hands into her pockets and waited for the ball to be returned. Between turns, we sat in orange molded-plastic chairs and retied our shoestrings. Whenever Max knocked down more than five pins, which was pretty often, he gave himself permission to go to the snack bar. Sometimes, his turn would come around and Maggie and I would wait for him, playing tic-tac-toe on the edge of the score sheet.

"It's about time," Max would say when he came back, still chewing a chili dog.

He didn't seem to give a whole lot of thought to the idea of bowling. I mean, it wasn't one of my obsessions or anything, but while I was playing, I tried to concentrate on the game. Max always came running back from the snack bar, complaining that he never had the time to get a decent meal. He would pick up whatever ball was sitting there, even if it weighed twenty pounds, and throw it toward the pins, straightening up with a little twist I swear he copied from Bruce Springsteen.

"Hungry?" my dad asked after the third game.

"Not especially," Max said, burping.

He'd already eaten two chili dogs, nachos, and a large orange soda.

"I could go for some ice cream," he said.

"Sushi," Maggie said, and her father smiled at her.

"Raw fish is not something I crave," I said.

"It's good for you," my dad said.

"I guess we could do a pizza," John said.

"Great," Maggie mumbled.

"Get anchovies on it if you have to," Max said to her.

"Are you ever quiet?" Maggie asked him. "I mean, do you have something to say about everything?"

Max shrugged and didn't say anything.

◇　　　　　◇　　　　　◇

The restaurant was one of those café-type places with a garden room, and no tables big enough for six people. Max, Maggie, and I sat together on the opposite side of the room from the adults. Max tried to order a double martini and I thought the waiter was going to kill him. "Okay, okay," he said. "Perrier and a slice of lemon."

"Diet Coke," I said.

"You're eating pizza and drinking diet soda," Max said. "There seems to be a contradiction here."

"Sprite," Maggie told the waiter.

She seemed like the kind of person who would order Sprite—bright, cheery.

Maggie's dad and John and my father were across the room drinking beer and eating popcorn. John started throwing popcorn at Maggie's dad, and he opened his mouth and practically leaped out of his chair just to catch it in his teeth. Fortunately, no one else noticed.

"Where does your dad work?" I asked.

"He's self-employed," she said, as though it meant something. "He designs furniture for hotels and places like that."

"What about your mom?" Max asked. I was curious but not planning on quizzing her, in case she didn't have a mom or her mom had gotten run over by a bus or something.

"She lives in Richmond," Maggie said, and you could tell there was more to it than that.

"Drag," Max said. "I mean, Richmond. Boring."

We stopped talking. Someone came around and lit the little candle on our table. Immediately Max started playing with it.

"Do you have a medical problem?" Maggie asked him.

He looked up at her. His fingers were still in the candle, cooking like at a barbecue.

"Shit," he said, pulling them out, dropping the candle onto the table, and sinking his burned fingers into his water glass.

"They have drugs to keep people from being so hyper," Maggie said.

Max took his fingers out of the water and put them in his mouth.

"They thought he was hyper," I said. "But all the tests came out normal."

I turned the candle upright to keep the tablecloth from catching on fire and then looked over at my father's table. All of a sudden, almost like slow motion, John leaned over and kissed Maggie's dad. Crud crept up in the back of my throat. I coughed.

"Gross," Maggie said. "Totally gross."

For a second, I'd forgotten anyone else was around.

"Oh . . . my . . . God," Max said very slowly, his eyes bulging. "Am I seeing what I think I'm seeing?"

I kicked Max under the table. He kicked me back.

"Shut up," Maggie said. "Just shut up."

"Was that artificial respiration or something, tell me?"

"If you even think of telling anyone, you'll die," Maggie said to Max. "I'll make sure of it. You won't even be able to walk to school, because you won't have any legs."

She was talking like she knew Mafia hit men, like they were her best friends, like she, too, secretly was one.

"You're freaking," I said to her.

I was freaking, too. I mean, we were in a public place and this guy did just kiss Maggie's father right on the mouth in front of the whole world.

"Why don't you just tell me what the hell this is all about," Max said.

"It's too much," Maggie said, ignoring Max. "At home, it's one thing, bad enough, but where people can see."

She looked at me. I shook my head. I didn't know anything

about it and even if I did, I didn't want to.

"Talk to me," Max said.

"I can't believe I have to live with this shit," Maggie said.

"Why?" Max said.

"Why?" She glared at Max. "You're really incredible. What do you mean, why? Why do you live with your father?"

"My mother, my father, me, my brother, we're a family, we live together," Max said, all insulted, like Maggie really thought he was retarded, which maybe he was, I dunno.

"Well," Maggie said. "That's my father and that's my family."

She pointed across the room. Her father's boyfriend lifted up his beer glass and tilted it toward us like he was making a toast.

"I hate him," Maggie said.

"Sorry," I said.

"What are you sorry for?" Max asked, taking a huge slice of pizza onto his plate. "The guy's an asshole, it's not your fault."

Max took a big bite and with his mouth full of food turned to Maggie. "So, is your dad really a fag or what?"

She shrugged and tried to eat.

"I've never known anyone who had one in the family," Max said.

Maggie gave me a funny look that I pretended not to see. On the way home I sat in the front next to my father.

"Could you open the window a little?" Max said from the back. "I feel sort of nauseous."

I cracked the window and let a hurricane into the car.

"Thanks," he said, putting his face into the wind like a dog.

"Maggie's a nice girl," my dad said. "Very grown-up, composed."

"She goes to my school."

"She's a bitch," Max said. "Sorry, I mean a snob. I'm surprised she lowered herself enough to go bowling."

"Guess she didn't know you'd be there," my dad said, leveling Max. "Sometimes, people aren't what they appear to be."

"Her father," Max said. "How can a guy be like that?"

"Max," my dad said, looking at him in the rearview mirror and nearly clipping a Chevy on our left.

I was petrified my dad was going to look Max in the eye and say totally sincerely, I'm a faggot, too.

"You have to learn to be tolerant of people who are different from you. The world isn't all one shape," he said.

And I realized my dad and Michael had more in common than anyone knew.

"He kissed the guy," Max said. "Right on the mouth, not on the cheek. They're not related, it wasn't his birthday. I think he even enjoyed it."

The whole car was silent.

"Maybe next time we should try duckpins. I heard they make their own ice cream over there," Max said.

We pulled up in front of his house. Mr. Burka was in the front yard playing with a sprinkler, like he was trying to fix it. I tilted the front seat forward so Max could get out. He didn't even notice.

"Hi, Paul," Max's dad said. He walked toward the car. "How've you been?"

"Good, good, real good." My dad looked down at the gearshift before looking up at Mr. Burka. "And you?"

"Doin' all right," Max's father said. He leaned toward the car and gripped Max by the shoulders.

"Just took the boys bowling," my dad said. "It was real nice."

"Maybe I'll come along next time," Mr. B. said. "I miss that kind of thing. You, me, the boys."

My dad nodded.

"Bunch of fags," Max mumbled to himself.

Everyone heard it. My dad and I blushed.

"Well, see you later," Mr. B. said, stepping away from the car and steering Max toward the house.

"Yeah," my dad called after him. "Take care."

"Mr. Burka knows, doesn't he?"

My dad pulled up in front of our house. He nodded.

"Wonderful," I mumbled.

"You know, Jack," my dad said. "We're all human."

"That's profound," I said. "Truly. But you see, male humans don't normally kiss other male humans in restaurants in front of other, younger humans."

"I'm sorry about what happened. But I can't control other people's behavior."

"Guess so," I said, getting out of the car.

"Other than that, it was fun, wasn't it?"

He asked this like he was pleading for me to say I had a good time.

"Yeah, I suppose so. I didn't exactly think your Margaret was going to be my Maggie from school."

"She's very pretty."

"I know, believe me, I know. So does she."

I could hear Michael hammering. He was listening to the radio and trying to sing along with a girl who had a high-pitched voice. It wasn't working.

"I gotta do homework," I said. "I promised Mom I'd be back by eight."

"Eight!" my dad said. "Why didn't you tell me? It's almost nine-thirty. She'll blame me. Go on," he said, shooing me away.

I cut across the lawn. The grass was long and tickled my ankles.

◇   ◇   ◇

Monday morning the word FAGGOT was written down my locker in heavy black Magic Marker. I didn't even bother opening it to get my books. Instead, I walked away slowly, moving down the row of lockers as though I'd forgotten which one was mine. At the end of the hall, I pushed open the door of the boys' bathroom. Max was leaning against the blue-tile wall, trying to smoke a cigarette. He hadn't grasped the concept of inhaling, so the smoke just seemed to flow from the cigarette into his mouth and then back out again. I ignored the ten other people standing around, grabbed Max by the collar, and slammed him against the sink. His foot hit the bar at the bottom and water came out of the little jets like an outdoor fountain.

"What the hell," one guy said, jumping out of the way.

"I want to talk to you," I said to Max. His cigarette fell into the sink and sputtered out.

"That was my last one," he said. "I bummed it this morning. You owe me."

Still holding his collar, I pulled him into the far stall and slammed the door. Max fell onto the toilet.

"What's the problem. You know, you didn't have to hurt me."

"My locker," I said. "Did you see my locker?"

"Kind of," Max said.

"What's kind of? It's like the goddamned Goodyear blimp."

"I didn't do it," Max said.

"Somebody knows something, Max. I wonder how."

He didn't say anything. Mr. Matthews, one of the science teachers, kicked open the bathroom door.

"Cigarettes out," he said. "Now! Or I take you down to the office."

"Teacher," everyone screamed, and I could hear the sound of feet stamping out Marlboros.

"Everyone, out," Mr. Matthews said.

From the echo I could tell that he had actually walked into the bathroom, something teachers rarely do.

"Look," I whispered to Max. "I'm not a faggot."

"I know," he said.

"I don't want that stuff on my locker," I said.

Mr. Matthews banged on the bathroom stall. "I said, out."

"We're talking," Max said.

"Open the door," Mr. Matthews said.

I unlocked the door and walked out with Max at my heels.

"Morning," I said to Mr. Matthews. I'd been in his algebra class in seventh grade.

"What were you doing in there?" he demanded.

"Talking," Max said. "A private conversation. Is that okay?"

Mr. Matthews gave us a weird look. "There are plenty of places to talk, this isn't one of them. Get to class."

"Thanks, that was wonderful," I said to Max when we were out in the hall.

"Look, all I did was say something to Andrew about

Maggie's dad and the whole bowling thing. I thought it was weird, all right?"

"No."

"I'm sorry," he said. "It's nothing to get hyper about. If you want, you can use my locker until it wears off."

"It doesn't wear off," I said. "It's goddamned black Magic Marker, permanent."

We walked down the hall to my locker. The first bell rang and everyone disappeared into classrooms.

"Maybe you could cover it," Max said. We stopped at the locker. "Paint it black or something."

I worked the combination and took out a pile of books. On the top shelf was a red marker I'd used to make a map of China for history class. Max grabbed it and in big letters wrote, NOT A down the locker next to mine. It looked like whoever's locker was next to mine was declaring that he wasn't a faggot. It made things look worse.

"Charming," I said. "At this rate, there'll be a whole novel up there by the end of the semester."

I went down the hall toward my class.

"Hey, faggot," Dean DePhillips said when I tried to sneak quietly into homeroom. "You're late."

His feet were sticking out into the aisle. I deliberately stepped on them.

"Just a joke," he said. "Don't get mental."

"No joke," I said.

"Class begins at eight-fifty-three. It's nine-o-two. Why are you late?" Mrs. Stevens asked.

"I had some trouble with my locker," I said.

Half the class started laughing.

"I fail to see the humor," she said.

"So do I."

During history, I was doodling while Mr. Carroll went on about civil rights. I'd never realized that it was only twenty-five years ago that black people couldn't eat or sit wherever they wanted to. I was thinking about all the things people have said and done to black people and then all of a sudden I thought about my dad. I wondered if people did or said horrible things to him on account of being gay. I mean, whoever wrote *faggot* on my locker had gone out of their way to rub my wrong side, but what if it was true? What if I was a faggot, then how would I feel? I nearly started crying and had to put my head down on the desk just to get a grip.

Carved into the plastic fake-wood desk top was a heart with Jack + Maggie etched into it. I practically had a heart attack. I traced over the carving with my pen. I tried to think of which Jack and Maggie it was talking about. There were about four Maggies in my class, and one other Jack, a guy about nine feet tall, with a major mustache. I had no idea of who'd carved it, but I wanted it to be my Maggie and me. I felt crazy, wild inside. I didn't want anyone to see it and at the same time I wanted everyone to know.

"I hate you," Maggie said when she passed me in the hall on her way to lunch.

I'd seen her coming out of the French room and was planning to say hi, and maybe ask her if she would be willing to go to a movie with me.

"You have an incredible lot of nerve," she said, and then stormed away before I could even figure out what she was talking about.

"Hey, lover boy," Max said when I sat down at the lunch table.

I glared at him and ate the four soggy Tater Tots on my lunch tray.

"Your name and Maggie's are scratched all over the place—walls, desks, even in the bathroom."

"I only saw one," I said.

"Well, there are about a thousand."

"Thanks for the news update. Who did it?"

Max shrugged. I figured he was guilty, at least in part.

Chris Culver leaned toward me. "Are you a fag or are you with Maggie?" he asked.

"He and Maggie are both fags," someone I didn't even know said, and then started laughing.

"From what I hear," Andrew said, "it's Maggie's father and your dad that are the hot item." He dropped his lunch tray onto the table, causing his Tater Tots to roll.

Max quickly picked up the loose taters and stuffed them into his mouth. "Jack, you tell us," Max said, making his carrot stick into a microphone and sticking it into my face. "What's the real story here?"

I bit the carrot, chewed it up, and spit it back into Max's face. Little pieces of chewed orangeness stuck all over him, and I was pleased. Max didn't make any effort to clean his face. We all sat in silence for about three minutes; everyone was sort of paralyzed by my sudden attack of Maxness—another word for the moment when a previously normal person suddenly has no impulse control. I drank my milk and burped.

I could see Maggie sitting with her friends on the other side of the room. They were looking at my table and trying not to be caught doing it. When I saw Maggie get up to drop off her tray, I got up and walked toward the garbage cans.

"I should have known," Ann McCormick said when I passed her table. I looked right at her braces as she said it; there was hot-dog roll pressed deep into the metal.

"What about it, lover boy," someone I didn't know said, and then pushed me directly into Maggie. "Why don't you talk to your girlfriend, fag baby?"

My tray knocked into Maggie's, and a thousand little pieces of corn went flying.

"Sorry," I said, and I dumped the rest of my tray into the trash.

"Fag baby, fag baby, fag baby," people behind me were chanting.

"Who do you think you are?" Maggie said to me.

Lunch was almost over and people were leaving the cafeteria.

"Excuse me?"

"I go bowling with you, your dad, and that creep." She pointed to Max, who was walking toward us. "And then today, all over school, Maggie and Jack. They were singing it to me this morning on the bus."

"Fag baby, fag baby," Richard Leonard said into my left ear, over and over again.

I elbowed him in the stomach.

"Fag baby, baby," he yelled in my face, and then ran away.

"Kids, kids, no fighting," Max said. "This is a room for higher education."

"Fag baby," someone walking by mumbled on the way out.

"I am not a faggot," I screamed. I turned to Maggie. "Just now, when I was trying to eat my lunch, someone tells me that the real hot news is that my dad is going out with your dad."

The people standing around were starting to listen.

"It's not true," Maggie said.

"No shit, Sherlock," Max said. "His dad's my godfather."

Maggie looked at Max. "What do you think Bob is?" she asked him.

"Who's Bob?" Max said.

"The guy who lives with his father?" Maggie said in a snotty tone.

"Shut up," I said to both of them.

"Oh, yeah, his roommate," Max said.

"You are so dumb," Maggie said.

"I'm going home now." I started to walk away. "I'm calling my mother and telling her I'm dying and that she should pick me up now. I'm sick, very sick. I think I have to transfer to another school."

Max followed me out the fire doors, leaving Maggie standing there, all annoyed.

"Is it true? Is your dad, is he, you know?" Max made his wrist limp and started walking like he was deformed.

I went into the nurse's office.

"Are you really a fag baby?" he asked.

"I have to go home," I told the lady in pink stripes, who wasn't really a nurse but liked to fake it.

"Do you have a fever?" she asked.

I shook my head. "I feel nauseous and sort of dizzy."

"Are you going to faint? Maybe you should lie down." She pressed her hand to my forehead.

"No, I've had this before. I think I should call my mom."

The pink lady looked up her number at work, which I could have just told her; I didn't feel good but it didn't mean I had Alzheimer's.

"He says he's sick to his stomach and dizzy," she told my

mom. "He says it's happened in the past."

The pink lady nodded a few times while my mother talked, then handed me the phone.

"Don't go home," Max said. "I don't care about your dad. It's like your locker. It's just a joke. Don't leave me alone in this awful school."

"Hi, Mom," I said. "Please pick me up now."

"Are you sick?" she said. "Jack, what's going on? I have a house to show this afternoon."

"Mom, pick me up or I'll walk," I said, like walking home was a real threat.

"Can't you just stay there for a while? Maybe they'll let you lie down—put the nurse on the phone—and then you can take the bus home with everyone else."

I imagined everyone on the bus chanting fag baby the whole way home.

"Mom, pick me up now." I was starting to get hysterical.

"Don't you have to go to class?" the pink lady asked Max. "Your friend will be all right now."

"I have to wait. His father is my godfather," Max said, like it was a good reason for skipping class.

I handed the phone back to the lady. She talked to my mom for a minute, then hung up.

"Sign out in the office," she said, handing me an early-dismissal slip.

I signed out and then went to wait on the front steps. Max followed me.

"So what," Max said. "So what if he's queer? I don't care."

"He sleeps with Bob, his roommate. They do things to-gether," I said to gross Max out.

"I sleep with my dog," Max said.

"Do you have sex with your dog?"

"You are so sick," Max said.

"Look, my father's gay, so is Maggie's and that guy John and Bob and about a million other people that we don't even know. They write *faggot* on my locker and they don't even know what it means."

I turned my face away so Max wouldn't see me crying.

"Maybe it's just a thing, you know, a phase," Max said, and then paused. "He hasn't tried to make you queer, has he?"

I wiped my face with my sleeve. "It's not a phase. I asked my mother. And you can't *make* a person queer. They either are or they aren't."

"Well," Max said. "You know how sometimes you think you know something and then it turns out that you don't? I do that all the time. I'm always wrong."

"Max, shut up," I said. "It's not something I dreamed. It's not a game. My father's a faggot. He took me out on the lake, he rented a rowboat, and out there, in the middle of the goddamned lake, he told me he's queer."

"So, what do you want me to do about it?" Max demanded.

"Nothing," I said.

We were quiet for a minute. The door behind us opened. We turned around.

"What's going on here?" the vice principal said. He came out onto the steps and stared at us.

"Waiting for my mother," I said, flashing my leave-early sick note.

"And you?" the V.P. asked Max.

"Waiting for his mother."

"Where's your pass?"

"He didn't feel good, and I didn't want him to be alone."

"You should be in class," the V.P. said.

Max stood up, and the V.P. pushed him back into school.

"Don't play games with me," the V.P. said.

◇　　　　　◇　　　　　◇

"**W**hat's the problem?" my mom asked when I got into the car.

I shrugged.

"Sore throat?" she asked.

I shook my head. I was about to cry.

"You don't want to talk about it, something personal?"

I nodded. "I'm dead meat," I said.

"Your father called after you left this morning. He wants you to come for dinner tonight."

"I don't want to."

"I told him to pick you up around six."

"Someone wrote *faggot* on my locker. The whole school knows. Dad's friend's kid that went bowling with us is in my class."

"She isn't in a position to talk," my mom said.

"It was Max," I said. "Just watch, at the next PTA meeting they'll announce it: GAY FATHERS COME OUT AT ROLLING HILLS JUNIOR HIGH. I can see the headline in the school paper."

"Who goes to PTA meetings anyhow?" my mom said.

"Don't make fun of me, okay, just don't."

"I apologize," she said. She reached over and ran her hand through my hair. "You need a haircut."

"Both hands on the wheel, please."

"Hair just like your father's. No matter what you do with it, long or short, it does something else."

"I don't want to have dinner with him. I don't want to see his apartment. I don't want to see Bob."

"Jack."

"I don't."

"He's not something to be ashamed of."

"They're tormenting me. They're calling me a faggot."

"Some people spend their whole lives trying to figure out what will make them happy. Your father realized that things weren't working and he did what he had to do to make his life right for him. Some men would have stayed home and made everyone miserable. He took a risk."

"What about you? He left you."

"I know. But I'm not doing so bad. I have a career. I didn't have one five years ago. I have the house, you, Michael, my friends."

"Are you happy?"

She shrugged. "I might not be happy even if I were happy."

"You sound like Michael, and sometimes Michael sounds like Dad, and sometimes you all sound like you're nuts."

She laughed. "He's making spaghetti for dinner," she said.

On the way home, we stopped to pick up the cleaning and some stuff at the grocery store, and by the time we got to the house Max was already there, sitting smack in the middle of the driveway, just asking to be run over.

"Hit him," I said.

My mother beeped, and finally he moved.

"I don't want to talk to you," I said as I got out of the car.

He followed me into the house and up the steps. We passed Michael in the hall.

"Some girl called you. She said she'd call back," Michael said.

"Thanks."

"It's Maggie," Max said. "She likes you."

"She practically spit in my face today. She said I was disgusting."

"She was referring to me," Max said. "She really likes you."

"Shut up."

"I think you've got her in the palm of your hand. I bet she'd even sleep with you if you play your hand right."

"You're deranged. And it's 'play your cards right.' You can play the harmonica, but there's no way you can play your hand. Besides, she hates me, she hates you, both of us."

"I don't think so, she called you."

"The Salvation Army calls, the Retarded Children call sometimes, too, but it doesn't mean it's the right number."

"Girls don't normally call people."

"Jack," my mom yelled up the stairs. "Wear something nice to dinner, all right?"

I didn't answer. The telephone rang.

"Jack," my mother yelled up the stairs, "telephone."

"I'm outa here," Max said, jumping up off my bed and running downstairs.

I picked up the phone in the hall.

"Look," Maggie said. "Your friend Max is a rodent, but all the other stuff about your dad, well, you know?"

I didn't say anything.

"I'm sorry, all right."

"Yeah," I said.

"I said, I'm sorry. You don't have to be all righteous about it."

"I'm not," I said. "Only it's not you that's the official fag baby."

"Well, I'm sorry." There was a silence. "I'm sorry I yelled

at you about the desks. I thought . . ." She didn't finish the sentence. "So, do you want to go to a movie sometime?"

I heard my father's car pull up out front. He beeped.

"What?" I said.

"God, a movie. Do you want to go to a movie?"

"Yeah, sure. When?"

"I don't know. Friday."

"Okay," I said.

And she started telling me about what was playing and what was supposed to be good and my father beeped again and my mom started yelling.

"I got to go," I said. "My ride's here. Can we talk later?"

"Fine," she said, and hung up.

It was the kind of "fine" that means it isn't fine at all.

◇   ◇   ◇

I changed my shirt real fast and ran out to the car. My father's apartment is in one of those developments with about a million other buildings that all look so much the same they have to number everything just so you don't get lost. We parked and went up the stairs. As we started going up, I got nervous. I wasn't going to my father's house, I was going to a gay person's apartment, and it was like I didn't know what to expect or how to behave. Plus on top of it Bob was going to be there. And the thing was, I knew Bob from before, when he was a regular person, but now it was weird because he was my father's lover.

By the time we got up to my dad's, I was having an authentic nervous breakdown, on top of starving to death and being totally out of breath. I'm not exactly used to walking up fifty thousand steps a day.

"We're home," my dad said when he opened the door.

"In a minute," Bob said from somewhere inside the apartment.

Since he'd moved out, my dad had lived in something like five apartments and two houses, but I'd never been to this one before. There was tan wall-to-wall carpeting and a lot of old wooden furniture that I figured was antique.

I was in his house and all I kept thinking about was him being gay and this being his house. Somehow everything in it was wrong or bad because it was gay, too. I didn't want to see it, know about it, or have anything to do with it.

"Carpet came with the place, the furniture's Bob's."

The worst part was there was nothing to see or not see, it was all perfectly normal, which was confusing as hell, considering.

"Where's all your stuff?" I said.

I was specifically referring to a sofa that he'd taken from our house even though my mom didn't want him to.

"In the den, I'll show you." He led me around the corner. "This is the hall and this is the bathroom," he said, opening a door.

"No kidding."

It annoys the hell out of me when people say, This is the kitchen, and this is the bathroom. What am I, Helen Keller? I mean, it's pretty obvious when you're in a kitchen and when you're not.

"And this is the den," he said.

He opened the door and inside was all the furniture he'd hijacked from our house—the sofa, some chairs, and other stuff I'd pretty much forgotten until I saw it sitting there, lumped together in one room. It was a little pathetic that he had all his stuff smushed together and Bob's was spread out all over the place. But, in a way it meant there was hope, there was some part of him that didn't completely belong to Bob.

"Maybe you'll come and stay sometime," he said. "The couch in the living room opens into a bed."

"Maybe," I said.

We walked back down the hall toward Bob, who was just sort of standing there. The closer we got the more convinced I was that I couldn't take it, I couldn't deal with it. I felt like I might pass out or something. I told myself to focus on something concrete. I zeroed in on Bob.

He looked normal enough except for his feet. He had red slippers on. Actual slippers, red leather with black trim, the kind of thing you see in Saks Fifth Avenue Christmas catalogs, or pictures of really old movie stars like Errol Flynn and stuff. Who the hell wears slippers, especially ones like that?

His hair was cut too short. I realized that every time I saw Bob his hair looked like it'd been cut that day. It always looked like if he left it alone it would get better in a few weeks, only he never left it alone. I wondered if he had a weird thing about hair.

I always notice people's hair. I think it's because my grand-father used to be a barber and every time I ever saw him he would go around saying something about taking a little off the top, needing some height, or maybe a good shaping.

"Hi, Jack," Bob said, patting me on the back.

He was patting me on the back and giving me one of those completely condescending looks my grandmother uses when she wants me to know that she knows something about me that's supposed to be personal. Obviously, my dad had told him about our afternoon at the lake.

"Hi," I said, kind of turning green.

I looked at Bob and hated him. I hated him for wearing

queer slippers, having hair that was too short, and doing whatever he was doing to my dad. It was horrible. I always used to like Bob, not a lot, but enough, and now I couldn't even look at him.

The way Bob was patting me on the back and looking down at me like I was an idiot made the whole thing with my father real. All of a sudden I got it together and finally understood that he was seriously involved with my father.

"Does this place have a balcony or anything?" I asked.

I felt nauseous as hell and needed a strong breeze or maybe a hurricane right in the face to cure me.

"Yeah, sure," Bob said. "We have a terrace."

I followed him into the living room, studying him, trying to figure why anyone, especially my dad, would be attracted to him.

Bob slid open the door to the balcony, and I stepped outside, bent over the railing and into the wind.

"Be careful," my dad said.

Same old Dad, I thought, imagining him dialing 911 and telling them that his son was out on the balcony of an apartment he shared with his gay lover, bent over the railing, breathing deeply.

I took a couple extra deep breaths and went back inside. Bob was setting the table.

"Playing a lot of basketball?" he asked me.

"Not as much as before, but I'm still on the team."

I could barely talk. There was a strange sensation in my throat, sort of painful, like a Life Saver was stuck there.

"I had to get a math tutor," I said.

I didn't want Bob to know I didn't like him. I figured having a conversation would make me seem a little more mature than he seemed to think I was.

"You never had a problem with math before," my dad said, sounding all upset from in the kitchen.

"It gets harder as you get older," I said.

"Jack, why didn't you ask me? You know I'd be happy to help."

"It wasn't my idea. The counselor at school set the whole thing up. No big deal."

I couldn't tell my dad that the whole reason I used to be okay in math was because I always sat next to Walter Thomas and he let me copy off his tests, but Walter moved to Ohio and abandoned me in Algebra One, Part Two.

"Other than that, how's school?" Bob asked.

I could tell he was making what he considered a big effort to talk to me. I wished he wouldn't. I wanted to hate him for a while longer. All the same, I knew if I mentioned the fag-baby stuff, it would bring everything to a crashing end, so I just shrugged.

"You and Max still best friends?"

I was looking at Bob, thinking, I don't know this guy. I was standing there, trying to hate him, like he was part of my family, maybe a distant cousin I only saw on holidays, someone I didn't know anything about except that we were related and that was enough. But I didn't know anything about Bob. His parents could be ax murderers; he could be one, too, and I'd never know. I kept telling myself he was a lawyer and that meant he was okay. Then, I remembered that everyone hates lawyers.

I was a complete vegetable, a zucchini-head. My dad liked him, supposedly loved him; did he love him more than me? I was looking at Bob and he was looking at me and I didn't know what the hell was going on.

"Bring him over sometime," Bob said.

"Who?"

"Max," Bob said. "I remember my best friend from junior high, Anthony McDaniel. Like Siamese twins, my mother used to say. On weekends we stayed up and watched all-night movies. We'd be sprawled out on the carpet in the den, eating potato chips and drinking Dr Pepper. Then we'd fall asleep and in the morning the TV would be turned off and all the empty Dr Pepper bottles and potato-chip bags would have been picked up and taken away like magic by my mother."

"Sounds like fun," I said, only because Bob was pouring out his whole goddamned life, and I didn't know what I was supposed to do with it. Plus, I was feeling a little paranoid. Why was he telling me this stuff? Did he know I thought maybe he was related to Charlie Manson? Was he trying to make me like him or what?

"Dinner," my dad said.

His voice sounded familiar and nice and kind of brought me back to earth.

"Great spaghetti." I heaped noodles and sauce onto my plate. "Real good," I said, thinking about the leftover spaghetti I'd eaten for breakfast. "I always love spaghetti." It sounded like I was trying to convince myself that it was true.

"So, how's things with you and Maggie?" my dad asked. "Maybe you should ask her out sometime. It would be nice for you to have someone to talk to."

He didn't mean "talk to" and I knew it. He meant he wanted me to have someone I could compare notes about this gay-dad stuff with, only he was too polite or shy to come out and say it.

"She already asked me out," I said.

My dad made one of those fake well, well, faces like I was

Don Juan or something, only it was really weird and extrafake because we both knew it wasn't like that.

"Details have yet to be arranged. Don't hold your breath for a wedding date," I said, playing along.

"You shouldn't get married anyway," Bob said, twirling his spaghetti around on his fork. "You're way too young."

I looked at him and couldn't tell if he was kidding or not, so I let it slide.

After dinner, I cleared the table. While I was loading the dishwasher, I could hear my dad and Bob talking in the dining room. Their voices were soft and I couldn't be sure of what they were saying. I could hear them talking like you hear an ocean from about a block away and I started thinking about the time my dad, Bob, and I had gone to Annapolis and taken a boat out to St. Michael's—this little town that you'd think was an island on account of how you take a boat there, but it's really attached to land somewhere. Anyway, the water was rough and a couple of people, including my dad, threw up over the side. When we finally got there, we walked around the town for a while and then went to a restaurant that stuck out over the water and we ate about a hundred hard-shell crabs. I remembered buying my mom an "I love St. Michael's" T-shirt with a red heart in place of the word *love*. It was a long time ago. You couldn't pay me to buy that shirt now. All the same, my mother wore it. She wore it until it had holes, and then tore it into dustrags. I didn't know if my dad and Bob were lovers then—it had never crossed my mind—but thinking back about it, I didn't think so. I finished loading the dishes and went back into the dining room.

"Want some dessert?" Bob asked. "We have carrot cake."

Seriously, is carrot cake dessert? I don't think so. I mean, it's nice, but a hot-fudge sundae is dessert. If someone's got carrot cake they should just ask, Do you want some carrot cake? instead of getting your hopes up for something good.

I nodded and Bob cut me a thick slice. We ate quietly, and then Bob got up to leave.

"Sorry," he said, to me, like my dad didn't matter. "But I have a meeting downtown."

"It's okay," I said.

"See you," my dad said, and I felt relieved as hell that Bob just walked out and they didn't kiss good-bye or anything.

My dad and I sat at the dining-room table, picking the crumbs off our plates with our fingers and then licking our fingers clean.

"So, how's everything at home?" he asked.

"Okay."

I always say okay. Sometimes I think my vocabulary is limited to about two hundred words.

"What about Mom? Is she working a lot? She shouldn't try and do so much. I worry about her."

"You do?" I was seriously surprised. If he was so worried about her, why the hell did he do what he did and all that?

My dad nodded and ran his finger around the bottom of the carrot cake, scraping off the white icing, the best part.

"I didn't think you thought about her at all."

"Jack," my dad said, surprised.

"Well, you left her," I said.

"That doesn't mean I don't care."

"Yeah, but now you have Bob."

We didn't say anything for a while. I cleared the cake plates and put them into the dishwasher. My dad came into the kitchen and hopped up onto the counter. He always used to do that at home, and my mom would yell at him.

"I don't dislike your mother."

"You don't seem to like her much either."

"That's not true."

"Well, you don't act like it."

"And when did you get to be the judge?"

I didn't answer.

I was sitting in my gay father's kitchen looking at things like the dish towels and the spice rack and wondering what the hell they meant. Lots of people have spice racks, don't they? I was worried that maybe I was going a little crazy, but there was no way to be sure.

"Look, Jack, it's true I left, but I still have a lot of feeling for your mother. You can't spend a big chunk of your life with a person and then not have feelings for them."

"What kind of feelings?"

"I love her," he said, and then stopped for a minute. "She's a very special person. That's why I married her. She's a good friend, you know that, someone you can talk to. She's an excellent mother."

"How come you never tell her that?"

"What?"

"Why don't you tell her she's a nice person or that you think she's a good mother. I never hear you guys say nice things to each other. You seem like you hate her or something."

"I don't hate her at all. Don't even say that. *Hate* is a horrible word. It's not that simple. She has a lot of feelings about me, you know."

"I know, believe me, I know."

"I don't think she especially likes me."

"She used to love you."

"Come on, Jack."

"I'm serious," I said.

We stood there kind of stuck and just stared at each other for a while. I couldn't believe I was having this conversation with my father. I was talking to him like I was his guidance counselor. I was giving him hell like he was my brother or my friend or something.

"What are you thinking about?" He always asked questions like that when he couldn't think of anything to say but didn't like the silence.

"Breathing. In through the nose, out through the mouth. Michael taught me. It's yoga."

"Nice guy—they get along well?"

"I guess." I paused. "She gets upset a lot. Michael says it's from holding things in. A lot of it's your fault."

I was being mean and I liked it. I wanted to go on and be meaner. I had this urge to tell him everything, all the horrible things that happened when he wasn't around to take care of things.

"You hurt her a lot." I stopped. "And me, too."

"Jack," he said.

I cut him off. "It's not exactly fair. You go do this thing of yours, find yourself or whatever, and then come back and expect everyone to knock themselves out understanding you."

"I don't expect anything," he said.

"They call me fag baby at school." I blurted it out, without really meaning to.

He didn't say anything for a while, but he really did look paler.

"Do you want me to go talk to them?" he asked.

"Talk to them, talk to who?" I said. "What do you want, a school assembly? Okay, everyone quiet now. Jack's father would like to talk to us about homosexuality and why we shouldn't call his son fag baby. You expect a goddamned lot."

"I'm sorry," he said. "I haven't been the greatest father and I probably was a lousy husband."

"You weren't a lousy father, that's the thing. You were the best."

"No," he said. "No one is. As much as I might have wanted to be."

"Wonderful. So, you do it for a while and then say, Sorry, I don't think I'm good at this. Oh, and by the way, I'm queer."

I blushed when I said the word *queer*. I felt the redness creep across my face like a rash and hated it.

"I know you're angry. You have a right to be upset."

"I'm glad I have your permission."

"I didn't plan to leave, not like that."

"But you did," I said.

We stopped talking and just sat there. I can be incredibly snotty when I have to. Finally, he picked up his basketball from the corner and threw it to me hard.

"Come on, let's shoot a few before it gets dark."

"That's okay," I said.

"I want to," he said.

He got up and started messing with the lock on the door. I threw the ball back to him.

"Look, Dad, I don't need you to play ball with me. Don't do it because you feel sorry for me or you think it will make me like you or something."

He looked hurt. "I asked you to play because I wanted to.

I don't get many chances anymore. Bob's about the worst athlete I've ever seen. Why the hell should I feel sorry for you?" my dad said.

He bounced the ball up and down on the floor until the people who lived underneath started yelling and banging on their ceiling. My father turned bright red. He does that sometimes.

"I keep forgetting this is an apartment."

"I'm not in the mood," I said.

"Come on," he said. He threw the ball across the apartment. I didn't catch it. I let it hit me square in the chest.

"Jack," my dad said.

"I have a game tomorrow, and Coach says we shouldn't exert on the day before."

"Shooting a few is not exerting."

"No," I said.

And we just kind of stood there, paralyzed. It was the kind of thing where in your head you're thinking so loud that you're sure you're actually having a conversation with the other person. Your thoughts are right there and you're telling them how you feel and the whole thing seems so real that in your head you can actually hear the other person talking back to you.

"Should I take you home?" my dad asked after what felt like a half hour.

He handed me my jacket. I put it on and walked out of the apartment. My father drove home real slow, like he wanted the ride to take ten years, like he wanted me to be grown-up by the time I got home.

"Look, Dad," I started to say.

"Forget it," he said. "It's okay."

An ambulance came up behind us, and my dad got flustered and pulled completely off the road into a ditch just to let it go by.

"Who're you playing tomorrow?" he asked as he rocked the car back and forth, grinding from reverse to first to get us up and out of the ditch.

"The Tigers."

"Are they the ones you nicknamed the psycho killers?"

I shrugged.

"I'd like to come to the game. I haven't seen you play for a while."

"Mom and Michael will be there."

"The gym should be big enough for the four of us."

"Everyone there will know you're gay."

"I think I can take it."

"They'll stare."

"So?" he said.

"It might not be a good idea."

"I promise I won't embarrass you. I'll dress real tough."

"Dad!"

There's no way to tell your parents what they can and can't do. You can try, but they don't hear anything once they've made up their minds. Once, my mother tried to take me to the father-son Scout dinner. She made me get all dressed up, and we even drove to the restaurant. The whole way there, I tried to explain what father-son meant. In the end, I refused to go in with her. So she went by herself and came out again about two seconds later, got back in the car, and said, "It's all fathers and sons."

"Dad," I said. "Do you remember the time we went to St. Michael's?"

"The crabs and the place on the water?"

"Yeah," I paused. "Were you and Bob, you know, lovers then?"

"No," he said. And then, like he was thinking about it some more, he said "No" again.

I was glad to have gotten something right for a change.

He pulled up in front of the house. "I want to go to your game tomorrow," he said. "But if you tell me I can't, I won't."

It was great—the power was all mine—but there's no way you can tell your dad he can't do something. Even if you don't want him to, you can't just come out and say, No, you can't. I mean, that would be a kick somewhere really important, like in the heart or something.

"I'm not going to tell you what to do," I said.

It sounded very grown-up, more mature than I actually was. I must have heard it in some movie or on a rerun of a TV show that went off the air about twenty years ago. Normal people don't talk like that.

"Thanks," my dad said.

"Look," I said. "I'm sorry I yelled at you before."

"You have good reasons to yell."

I sounded like an imaginary character, and my father sounded like a radio psychologist. He smushed me on top of the head like he used to do when I was little.

"It wasn't very nice of me," I said as I opened the door. "And just so you know, I don't totally hate Bob, but you should throw out his slippers sometime when he isn't looking."

"I'll be sure to tell him," my dad said.

I closed the door and started walking toward the house. As soon as I was sure my dad had driven away, I turned around and walked in the opposite direction. I was walking and thinking. Walking and thinking about a whole lot of junk, like what it means to be a family and stuff.

I know that my mom and my dad are my parents and everything, but sometimes I wonder if that means they're supposed to give up their whole lives just to be my parents. It sounds extreme, but when you think about it, kids take up a lot of time and seem to need things that I wonder if parents can really do.

I walked around the block a couple of times, wondering whether or not one day I might get married and have kids. I walked around the block and looked at all the houses. They all had lights on inside, and without even trying I could see what the people in them were doing. Twice, I passed our house and saw my mom talking on the phone and Michael in the living room reading.

It got cold out and little drops of rain started falling, and even though I wasn't half done thinking, I started running. I was running down the street and there were leaves all over the place and the rain made them slippery and there's no way in hell to run down the street trying not to break your neck and still think about whether or not you'd be able to change diapers and read stories and stuff.

◇   ◇   ◇

First thing the next morning, Coach got on the P.A. and in his foghorn voice announced a lunchtime pep rally followed by a short meeting of the basketball team. I don't have a problem with team meetings or anything, but pep rallies are embarrassing as hell and should be illegal, especially on the junior-high level.

What I'm trying to say is that I had to stand there in my dinky little uniform while cheerleaders ran all over the place, shaking and screaming, trying to get everyone all hot and bothered. And while they do their rah rahs, what really happens is that everyone sitting there starts checking out the physical development of the entire ball team.

I know it sounds like I'm going on about nothing, but it's true. Wearing your uniform at a game is one thing because everyone's concentrating on the game and you're moving around a lot so nothing's obvious. But, standing there in broad daylight in the middle of the gym is like being under an electron microscope. Everyone can practically count the hairs on your legs and stuff.

It's not even like I'm way behind; in fact I'm sort of ahead on account of how I'm older than a lot of the guys because my birthday was early or late or something and I was six when I started first grade. Sure, there are some guys on the team that are sixty feet tall and have more body hair than King Kong. I'm not one of them, but who would want to be? All the same, I didn't like standing there being looked at by two hundred people who liked to call me fag baby.

Coach's meeting turned into a lecture and I knew I'd be in trouble when I tried to sneak into Spanish class almost a half hour late. But Coach didn't care about stuff like that; he cared about the team and he cared about winning. We sat on the cold floor of the small gym with our backs pressed up against the pale green cinder block. Coach paced back and forth. His stomach pushed against the waistband of his blue polyester coach's shorts, causing the waistband to roll over and make a kind of shelf under his stomach.

"First and foremost, you're animals," he said. "Don't forget it. Your nature is to compete, to fight for what you want, and what do you want? To *win*," he shouted, stopping for a minute to adjust his crotch.

Coach had a terrible habit of constantly picking at his crotch. Even when he wasn't being Coach, even when he was Mr. Wallace, the biology teacher, he would sit there and dig at his crotch in front of the whole world like it was his divine right to gross everyone out.

"You're born knowing how to fight, how to kill, how to survive. But you've been trained to suppress your natural desire. Wake it up."

Everyone laughed. In junior high, desire equaled sex. Coach didn't get it and looked confused.

"I'm tired of watching you play ball like a bunch of faggots."

I pressed my back farther into the wall until I thought I might go through the wall.

"Are you faggots or are you animals?" he screamed.

What a jerk, I thought. First off, my dad could beat him in basketball in a minute, and second, what incredible idiot stands in a junior-high gym and tells twenty guys that if they don't kill, they're faggots. And you wonder why some people grow up and become mass murderers and stuff?

"You gonna fight to win?"

"Yeah," everyone shouted. I opened my mouth but didn't say anything.

"All right," he said, clapping his hands together. They made a loud snap that bounced off the walls and into my head.

"Be here at seven," he said as we all raised ourselves up off the floor, changed back into normal clothes, and raced to get to class. Maggie caught me in the hall and tried to make plans for Friday night.

"Can we talk later, at the game or something?" I said.

"I never go to games," she said.

"I can't talk," I said. "I'm thirty-three minutes late for a class where the teacher already hates me."

"Whatever," Maggie said.

She walked off without saying anything. Wonderful, I thought to myself. Instead of starting off on the right foot, I was tripping all over myself, all over the place.

Even though Coach had a rule about "saving ourselves" on a game day, as soon as I got home I picked up my basketball. It was low on air, but if I started hunting around for the air pump, by the time I got everything the way it should be, I wouldn't have been in the mood to play anymore. I ran around the driveway slamming the ball down hard, with my whole hand, instead of the Fast-Jack way with just my fingertips. The ball wouldn't bounce any higher than my knees, so I had to crouch way down in order to get any control. I kept telling myself that it was an exercise to develop upper-thigh and knee strength.

We ate dinner early so I could digest before the game. According to Michael, bad digestion is one of the major reasons for the state of the world today. He said bad digestion and hunger were the two root causes for all moral and political decay.

I was constantly tempted to tell him that I wasn't sure these things had a lot in common. I mean, how can starving people have trouble with their digestion? I never actually mentioned it because Michael probably had some three-hour theory about food, your soul, and human understanding achieved through the starvation of certain body systems.

"You want us to give you a ride to school?" my mom asked as we were doing the dishes.

"I have to be there early."

"Michael and I can hang out in the gym, maybe sneak

around a little, write on some desks, smoke a couple of cigarettes in the bathroom."

"They get very upset if you smoke in the bathrooms."

"I know," she said. "I was just kidding. You remember kidding?"

"I'll walk," I said.

"You know what Elaine Burka said to me today?" I shrugged. "She thinks you're special. She said there's something about you that's different from other people. I don't remember exactly what she called it, an understanding or something."

I nearly dropped my mother's good white platter. "Why'd she say that?"

"I don't know, we were just talking. She says it's always been there, ever since you were a kid."

I've always liked Mrs. Burka, the whole Burka family, Max included. I mean, they were sort of my ideal family—you know, mom, dad, two kids, and all. I used to want a little brother and stuff like that. There was something about Mrs. Burka—I can't explain—something that made her different from other mothers.

A moth banged against the back door again and again, and Michael and my mom started talking about their bank account.

"I better get my stuff together," I said as I walked out of the kitchen and up to my room, still thinking about Mrs. B. and my "understanding."

The locker room was filled with pregame talk. Coach walked through a couple of times while we were getting ready, and each time the whole place went silent. He looked us over, and I expected him to take a deep breath and tell us we were dog shit if we didn't win this one. But he didn't say anything, and the level of tension went up. Finally, he came out and blew his whistle. The sound echoed off the tiles like an explosion. We all jumped up off the wooden benches and stampeded up the steps into the gym.

> Blue and Gold
> Blue and Gold
> Are our Colors
> Bright and Bold.

The cheerleaders bounced in syncopated rhythms, shaking the gym floor. I felt dizzy and looked away from them, away from the bleachers, and down at the polished planks of blond wood.

> We're the Bulls
> Of Rolling Hills
> We're the best
> Of all the rest.
> Go. Guys go.

We lined up in strict formation to run warm-up eights. One guy dribbling a ball came in from the left, another ran in from the right. About halfway, the left fed the ball to the right, who put up the shot. The ball hit the backboard and the rim before falling through the net. The next pair was already in motion when our assistant team manager caught the ball under the net and threw it to a guy farther back in line.

It sounds retarded to describe in words, but in practice it's pretty damn graceful because both teams are doing the same thing and there are about ten balls all in motion and everyone's dancing around like they know exactly what they're doing.

The referee blew the whistle and we went back to our bench, all breathing evenly and coated with a thin layer of sweat. Coach sent in the starting five—I wasn't one—and the game began. My pulse was doing its usual double time and I felt the weight of the people in the bleachers pressing down on the bench. I wanted to turn around and see where my mom and Michael were sitting and who else was watching, but I was too nervous and so I sat, arms wrapped around myself, staring hard at the players like maybe my concentration would become theirs.

Near the end of the first quarter, Coach tapped me on the shoulder. There was a time-out and Greg Burkhard came running toward the bench. I stood and, just before stepping out onto the court, I looked back at the bleachers. My father and Bob were sitting behind the team bench, about four rows up.

I ran out onto the court, almost tripping over my feet. For the first couple of plays, everything seemed to happen too fast. I couldn't think, couldn't concentrate. I screwed up and let a couple of guys slip past me.

The Tigers had the ball. I forced my mind to be right. When one of them attempted to pass the ball to another, Mark Reed stuck his arm in just the right place and the pass was blocked. The ball bounced off Mark's arm and hit the floor right in front of me. I crouched low, curling myself around it, dribbling, almost patting the ball, spinning it backward so it wouldn't get ahead of me. Tigers closed in, keeping me from my teammates. I faked to the right and moved left, heading downcourt, sticking close to the line, hoping I wouldn't be forced out. Just as I was about to be nailed, Mark freed himself and I passed the ball upcourt about ten feet. Mark dribbled twice, took a single step, and hurled the ball high and clean. It sailed through the net with a thick swishing sound.

With each trip up and down the court, I turned more and more into Fast Jack. I could tell who was going to move where and when. Twice, I took the ball in myself, staying low, threading through Tigers until I was in a position to shoot. Both times, I was right on the mark.

During halftime I sat on the bench, bent over into myself. Coach patted me on the back and said I was playing good, "angry like a killer." I didn't want to hear it. My eyes were closed and I was in my head. I was in the park, alone under the lights, dancing with my Wilson. I could hear the cheerleaders all around me. I closed my eyes tighter and wished I could close my ears. My sweat was drying, sealing everything like Saran Wrap. I took a towel from the pile and ran it across my face and arms.

The buzzer went off. Coach jammed two fingers into the space between my shoulder blades and pushed me back into the game. It took a few minutes to get going again, to loosen the muscles. I fine-tuned my radar and leaned into the game, arms loose, torso ahead of my feet. We were ahead, 40–38. Tony White put up a shot that hit the place where the backboard and hoop meet. The ball stuck there for a second and then started to fall. I knew if I jumped I could put it up again, push the ball a little higher, harder, so that it would hit the backboard and fall through the net.

I bent my knees and pushed off the floor. As I rose I felt a Tiger rise with me, his body pressing against mine, threatening to tower over me, to slam the ball down. I stretched, cupping my right hand under the ball. At the height of my jump, I caught the ball and pushed it back up toward the basket. I turned my head away as I started to fall. The Tiger twisted into me, and for a second our bodies both took up the same space. As we landed, my left leg got tangled in his right. I came down unevenly on my right foot. It turned under, the ankle gave way, and pain, long and wide, ripped through my leg. I fell hard onto the floor.

"Jack." I heard my father's voice echo through the gym. I opened my eyes and saw Coach lumbering toward me. My father was right behind him. I tried to get up. Tony White grabbed my elbow. "Jack," my father said, taking my other arm. Together, they lifted me into the air.

Guys fall down all the time during a game, and mostly their fathers know better than to go running out on the court. I put my hurt foot down and again the pain ripped through.

"Is it broken?" my dad asked—like, what am I, a doctor?

I shook off my father and Tony and walked back to the bench, determined not to limp, not to show how much it hurt.

My father followed me. "Let me see," my father said.

He and Coach were leaning over me. I could feel Coach's stomach pressing over his pants and into my shoulder. It felt like the whole gym was watching. I looked through the space between Coach and my dad, at the scoreboard: We were up by four; the shot was good.

"It's all right," I said, stretching my leg out in front of me, hoping it would prove something.

Coach turned around, tapped Tom Rusk on the shoulder, and sent him into the game. They started playing again. My father bent down on his knees and started to untie my sneaker string, like I was an infant that didn't know how to.

"Stop it," I said.

He held on to my shoe until I pulled my foot away from him. "Please just go and sit down," I said.

He pressed his hand onto my leg, left it there for a minute, and then crawled back up into the bleachers. I watched him go and looked around for my mom and Michael. They were way in the back, in the top row on the other end of the gym. My mother had a terrible expression on her face, like she wanted to come down and see how I was, but she didn't know how to get there without making everyone in the gym stand up to let her through. I sort of tried to smile so she would know I wasn't dying or something.

Roger Mudrick brought me one of those Shake'n Bake-type cold packs. You snap a little tube in the middle and some chemical squirts out into this plastic pouch of blue jelly, then you shake it around a little and the whole thing gets freezing cold. I took off my sneaker and sock, and wrapped the cold blue around my ankle.

I tried to get back into the game, mentally. At the beginning of the fourth quarter we were tied; by the middle we were losing. I could feel the team getting tired; their strides were shortening as they ran the court.

I wanted to go in. I wanted to dance with the Wilson on the blond floorboards. I pressed my foot into the floor, as if to stand. The pain that flew up from my foot and stopped at the back of my throat just short of a scream seemed to say that I wouldn't be dancing with anything for a while. When the buzzer went off, the Tigers had won 82–68.

◇   ◇   ◇

"Can you walk on it?" Coach asked as the game broke and everyone headed back to the locker room.

"I don't think so," I said, trying not to seem like a major wimp.

My dad and Bob, my mom and Michael all came over while Coach was trying to figure out what to do. Somehow they acted like Coach should know what to do, as if Coach should be used to guys practically killing themselves under his direction. But even though Coach—Mr. Wallace—may have been a biology teacher, he wasn't a doctor and he wasn't the smartest guy in the world, if you know what I mean. Most schools have a team doctor, but ours got arrested for shoplifting or something truly charming like that.

"There's some crutches downstairs somewhere," Coach finally said, heading off toward the locker room.

I saw my mom and Bob looking at each other, but not knowing what to say. I was totally freaked that no one knew what to do. I mean, what if I were dying. Would they have just stood there, watching?

"Mom, this is Bob. Bob, this is Mom," I said. I was sitting there, with my leg in like twelve pieces, playing host.

"Hi," my mom said, sticking out her hand too fast, almost smacking Bob.

"Nice to meet you," Bob said, shaking her hand with both of his hands. "I've heard a lot of—" He paused like he had to make sure he was saying the right thing. "Jack talks about you," he said, blushing and not looking directly at anyone.

My mom nodded. "This is Michael," she said.

"I think we should run you over to the emergency room," my dad said.

"We can take care of it," my mother said, and even though she just meant he shouldn't worry, it didn't come out sounding very nice.

I sat there wishing there were a way to disappear. The gym

was empty, the game lights were off, the janitor was folding the bleachers. Everything looked old and faded.

"Jack," my dad said, "do you want me to take you to the hospital?" I shook my head.

"It'll be okay," I said. I wasn't sure it was true, but in spite of the fact that I was in incredible pain, I couldn't help but start thinking about all the times I used to want him for stuff and he wasn't there. I felt like telling him to get the hell away from me and stay away.

"You sure?"

"Positive," I said.

Bob gave me a long, sad look like I was a puppy in a pet-store window. I still hated him. I couldn't help it.

"Really, it's fine," I said, looking at the floor.

Coach came back with the crutches and we all stood around waiting while he tried to figure out how to adjust them, on account of how the last guy who sprained his ankle must have been Wilt Chamberlain or the Jolly Green Giant or something. Finally, Michael whipped out his Swiss army knife and fixed them in about two seconds.

Getting across the driveway was a pain, but no one offered to go get the car and I didn't feel like asking. The crutches were slow and it was dark. I couldn't see where I was going. In order to take a step, I had to put the crutch out in front of me, press down hard, and hope to hell I wasn't aiming for a pothole. Twice, I did it all wrong and caught myself from falling by bearing down on my busted foot. Both times my parents moved to catch me; both times they were too late and I had to catch myself.

As we got near Michael's VW, I could see his SAVE THE HUMANS bumper sticker throwing off little glittery sparkles under the streetlight.

"Keep it elevated," my dad said when we got to the car. "Ice for the first twenty-four hours and then heat. Do you have an ice bag? Take some aspirin as soon as you get home. Is there any in the house?"

"We can take care of it," my mom said.

"You're sure you don't want to go to the emergency room?" he asked.

" 'Night," my mom said, settling it, and then getting into the backseat, so I could have the front.

"Nice meeting you," Bob said.

My dad and Michael stuffed me into the car, and put the crutches in the back with my mom.

"He's getting weird," I said when we drove away.

"Same as always," my mom said.

I pulled down the visor and looked at her in the clip-on mirror. Every time a car passed us, light crossed through the backseat and I could see her face clearly, like it was in a movie or something.

"I don't think he knows I'm getting older. Fathers do not run out onto the court when their kids fall. Not anymore."

"He thought you were hurt."

"In two weeks I'll be starting driver's ed. Do you realize that?"

"Seems hard to believe," my mom said.

"No, it doesn't." I very definitely felt sixteen years old. Sometimes I felt like forty years old.

At home, in the bathroom, I pulled off my uniform and stood at the sink. I ducked my head under the tap and held it there while the cold water rushed around the backs of my ears. While I was combing my hair, I noticed that in the mirror, if I held my head a certain way, I looked just like Paul Newman did about a million years ago. I couldn't help but go with it. I opened the medicine chest, took out the aspirin, and in one flick of the wrist, knocked out two, perfectly, heads up. I tossed them into my mouth, the way I figured Newman would, only throwing the aspirin back, not my whole head. I swallowed the sour bits before the water, not with it, and then kind of grimaced just for effect. For a second I broke character; I was practically choking. I drank about a gallon of water, fast, on account of both aspirins seeming to have taken up permanent residence somewhere in my windpipe. My mother knocked on the door.

"I made you an ice pack," she said.

"Thanks." There was a pause.

"I think you should put your foot up."

"I will in a minute." I looked in the mirror and Newman was gone. It was just me with a sopping-wet body and goose bumps all over. The phone rang. I hopped into the hall and answered it.

"Are you okay?" Max asked. "I heard you broke your leg and your dad carried you off the court crying."

"He didn't carry me. I didn't cry, and it's not broken."

"Too bad I didn't get to see it."

"Yeah, too bad."

"Guess you won't be at school tomorrow."

"Doubt it," I said.

"Oh, well, I'll come over," he said, and then hung up before I got a chance to say anything, like Don't bother.

My mom wrapped my ankle with an ice pack made out of plastic produce bags filled with crushed ice. She stuffed about forty pillows under my leg so it was almost as elevated as the Empire State Building.

"I'll bring you some aspirin," she said.

"I already took two."

"I wish you were on the swim team. It's not so competitive. It's not dangerous."

"I might drown," I said.

◇   ◇   ◇

In the middle of the night, I woke up screaming. I must have started screaming in my sleep because by the time my eyes were open and adjusted and everything, my mom and Michael were already standing there staring at me as though I were possessed.

"We're going to the emergency room," Michael said. My mom pulled a sweatshirt on over my T-shirt, and Michael carried me out to the car. I probably could have used the crutches, but I was too tired to argue about it. I mean, what's pride in the middle of the night?

"What time is it?" I asked on the way to the hospital.

"Four-thirty," Michael said, leaning far into the dashboard to check the clock. The car crossed over into the opposite lane.

"Please watch the road. This is when the drunk drivers are out," my mother said.

I lay across the backseat, leaning against the door, which my mother kept checking to make sure it was locked and wouldn't fly open, sliding me out onto the highway.

"Just don't tell your father," she said. "Tell him that when we got home you decided to go to the hospital."

I nodded. There were no other cars on the road. The only lights on were random kitchen lights someone had forgotten to turn off, and porch lights that were supposed to keep burglars away.

"Maybe I should call him."

"Don't," I said.

Michael pulled up to the emergency entrance. It was red and glowing. Compared to the outside, compared to the night, the emergency room was lit up like the Fourth of July. Even though the place was empty, it took about a half hour to get waited on.

"Can you do this," the doctor said, twisting my foot one way and then the other, not waiting for me to answer. My ankle was stiff and hurt like hell. After the guy practically ripped my whole leg off, they X-rayed it, twisting it around and around like they were trying to unscrew it or something.

"It's not broken," the doctor finally said. And then he went out to the waiting room and got my mom. "We're going to put it in a cast for two weeks—torn ligaments, a bad sprain. I want it immobile." He turned to me. "You will walk again," he said.

It was really weird because it'd never occurred to me that I wouldn't and then all of a sudden I got scared that I was going to be a major cripple. I felt faint and had to put my head between my legs for a couple of minutes.

The doctor put his hand on my knee and squeezed it so hard that I thought maybe he was trying to break it so he could hike up the bill or something. He wrapped the bottom half of my leg with this plaster-gauze soaked in water. In fifteen minutes, it had dried so hard that when I knocked on it, my leg sounded like plywood.

"This is for the pain." The doctor handed my mom a prescription slip. "He should only need it for a day or two."

He squeezed my knee again when he was all finished. "Relax," he said. "Relax."

It was seven-thirty in the morning when we got home. My father's car was parked on the street in front of the house. He jumped out as we pulled up.

"I called and no one answered," he said. Michael carried me into the house and my father followed us in. It was the first time he'd been inside since he'd packed the green garbage bags. I wondered if he remembered.

"It's not broken," my mother told him.

"How long are you off your feet?"

"Two weeks," I said.

"I have three appointments this morning," my mother said. "But before I leave, I'll run over to the drugstore and get your prescription filled."

"I can get his prescription," my father said.

Michael was already putting on his heavy work boots and rummaging around for his gloves.

"I called Elaine from the hospital, and she said she'd come over and sit with you as soon as she dropped Sammy off at his school," she said.

"I don't need a baby-sitter."

I got up from the sofa and started hopping toward the stairs. I wanted to rip the goddamned cast off and run out of the room, out of the house. I started hopping, and Michael ran ahead of me and came back with the crutches. It was easier to pull myself up with the railing.

I lay on the bed, dead leg resting on a pile of pillows. My mom brought me a tray, complete with two flowers stuck in an old jelly jar. She brought me breakfast and then disappeared to get ready for work and to get the circles out from under her eyes. The doorbell rang about thirty times before she finally heard it and went down to let in Mrs. Burka and Max.

"It's just sprained," my mom said. "But he's in a cast for two weeks."

"Where's the cripple?"

Max pounded up the stairs like he was doing sound effects for an entire army.

"So, are you out for the count or what?"

He sat down at my desk and started messing with things as though it was really his desk and I'd just been borrowing it all along.

"Two weeks," I said.

"Two weeks and then two weeks—I know about these things." He picked up one of my crutches and started playing machine gun with it. "Guess you won't be in school for a while."

"Couple of days."

"Guess you won't be running around with Maggie for a while." He paused. "I mean, it would be pretty hard with your leg all amputated and everything."

All of a sudden, I remembered that we were supposed to go to the movies on Friday. I remembered that I'd promised to call her.

"Who knows," Max said. "Maybe she's into cripples. Maybe she'll want to play doctor."

"You're so, so spastic," I said. It was all I could come up with.

"Thanks, well, got to go. If I'm late one more time this year, I get sent to jail or suspended or something."

My mother brought me a pill and a glass of water. "Your father picked these up for you. He had to run to a meeting, but he'll call you later."

I took the pill. This time, there was no Paul Newman, it was just me, Jack, with my leg wrapped like a cocktail frank. My mom sat on the edge of my bed very carefully, like she didn't want to hurt me. She didn't say anything, just sat there looking at me as if she had to memorize the exact position of every freckle.

"Bye, sweetie, I have to go to work. Elaine's downstairs."

She said she was leaving, but then she just sat there watching me.

I felt tired as hell, from the game, from falling, from losing, and from the emergency room. I closed my eyes. My mother lifted herself off the bed, pushing down with her hands and sort of picking herself up, trying not to wake me.

"I'm not asleep," I said.

"Shhh," she said, kissing my head and tiptoeing out of the room.

When I woke up, the sun was seeping in around the edges of the shades. The house was quiet and hot. I lay in my bed, examining the floor and the way little fragments of light landed on the boards. Each piece of wood seemed enlarged, like under a microscope. I noticed the floor was worn. There were little dips in it, and places where the wood looked soft, without grain, almost white. I rolled my head around and looked at the walls. They also seemed different, gray, not white, maybe covered with a thin layer of dirt, fingerprints. The last time we'd painted them was last year, just after Michael moved in, but it seemed like that was a long time ago.

"How are you?" Mrs. Burka said. She was standing in the hallway just outside my room.

"Weird."

She stepped closer. "Your mom called at eleven, and your dad called about a half hour ago. Max called twice, and some girl named Ann McCormick, and then Maggie once. She sounds cute."

"What time is it?"

"Two-thirty. Are you thirsty?"

"I guess," I said.

Mrs. Burka disappeared, and I slid my legs over the edge of the bed, pushing myself up onto one leg, stork position. I shoved the crutches deep into my armpits and started down the hall. Mrs. Burka was downstairs. I heard her opening the freezer, then smacking an ice-cube tray down on the counter. In the bathroom I nearly fainted. I was standing there, going, and all of a sudden everything started getting black around the edges. One of the crutches fell and made a loud noise.

"Jack, are you all right?" Mrs. Burka asked.

Her voice sounded like it was pressed up against the door. I leaned back against the wall. The tiles were cool and somehow refreshing. Everything faded back to normal. A minute later, I opened the door, and Mrs. Burka helped me back down the hall and into bed.

"You look very pale," she said, handing me a Coke with crushed ice to sip.

"I feel very pale," I said, taking small drinks and then putting the glass down on the floor.

She reached out her hand, the fingers bent like the claws of a cat, and ran them through my hair, pushing it back like my grandmother used to do when I was about six. This time, it felt different.

"Do you want another pill?"

I shook my head. "They make me feel unconscious."

She ran her hand down my arm, like in that game where you try and figure when someone gets to the crack in your elbow. Her nails half scratched, half tickled me. I don't know if it was because of the pill I'd taken, but there was something incredible about it. If she hadn't been Mrs. Burka, Max's mom, I would have asked her to keep doing it, to do it to my whole body, for hours on end. I didn't say anything. I closed my eyes. She slipped her hand into mine and squeezed. I wondered if she knew how she was making me feel. I mean, normally mothers don't make a point of terrorizing young guys. I lay there, trying to concentrate on the pain that was starting to seep back into my leg. I held her hand. It wasn't like others—Ann McCormick's, Maggie's, my mom's, or even Max's. There was something traveled about it. The skin was clean, cool. The bones felt small and breakable. To be honest, it felt sexy. With my thumb I could actually feel the veins on the top of her hand.

"Your mom should be home soon," she said, her hand still in mine.

For a couple of minutes I was totally deranged. Some warped part of me had the idea that she was feeling the same as I was and that the "mom should be home soon" was a message. I didn't know if it meant hurry up and make a move or cool out.

"She said, she hoped by three," Mrs. Burka said.

I could feel her watching me. I opened my eyes.

"If she's not back by three-thirty, I'm going to have to run out and pick up Sammy. Do you think you'll be okay?" I nodded. "It'll only be about twenty minutes." I sipped some more Coke.

"How's your leg?"

"Hurts," I said.

Just as Mrs. Burka was getting ready to leave, my mom came home. I heard her car in the driveway, the door shutting, and then her voice and Mrs. Burka's running together as they talked softly downstairs. The phone rang. When my mother answered, Mrs. Burka left. From upstairs, my mother's voice sounded a little bit like music. Not regular music, but the avant-garde stuff Michael sometimes listened to. I mean, I couldn't really hear her words, but the tone and rhythm stayed the same. She said something, paused, then said some more. Finally, she hung up, turned on the water, and then answered the phone again when it rang. As soon as she hung up, the phone rang again. "Shit," she said loudly before she picked it up.

Awhile later, she hung up and came upstairs. "Hi, sweetie," she said, kissing my cheek and rubbing my forehead like she was checking to see if I had a fever or not.

"Who keeps calling?"

"First your coach—what an idiot. Then your father wanted to know if I needed him to come over." She said this as though she didn't really believe it.

I couldn't blame her. I mean, for two hundred years I couldn't even get him to drive into the driveway; now all of a sudden he wanted to come over.

"I said you were fine and that you didn't need him, but if he wanted to come he was welcome. He said he had a lot of work to do but would call you later. Then Max called to ask if he could bring Maggie and a pizza over. At first, I thought Maggie was the pizza, but then I remembered she's the girl you like."

"Mom!"

"They should be here in about forty-five minutes. How do you feel?"

"Fine." I looked down at myself. I was still wearing the T-shirt and shorts I'd put on last night. "I have to change," I said. I was thinking about the leg that wasn't in a cast, my skinny leg, covered with freckles that Max promised would turn into skin cancer in a few hundred years.

"Jeans won't fit over the cast," my mother said. She was cool, calm, and collected. She didn't have a crush on Maggie. She hadn't just spent the afternoon with Mrs. Burka tickling her arm. She was probably tired from work.

"Sweats," I said.

My mother handed me a pair, a clean T-shirt, and brought a wet washcloth in from the bathroom so I could kind of get it together. I could have gone in there myself and washed my own stupid face, but Mrs. Burka must have told her about my nearly passing out.

◇   ◇   ◇

"Hey, cripp," Max said, breezing into my room with a large pizza box.

"Hi," Maggie said, following him, but hanging back a little.

"Come in," I said.

"Your leg looks broken," she said.

"It's not. I only had them put it in a cast because casts are very hip. And what can I say, I'm a trendy guy."

"She knows that you planned the whole thing so you don't have to take her out on Friday," Max said.

I blushed.

"Not true," Maggie said.

"Whatever." Max parked himself at my desk in front of the pizza and started eating.

My mom brought up some Cokes and paper plates. I could tell she was kind of checking Maggie out, looking at little stuff like her sneakers, to see if the laces were tied or if they were totally falling apart and held together with electrical tape or something, as though that would say a lot about the person.

I looked at Maggie's feet. Her sneakers were fine—clean,

white, with black-and-white-striped laces, cute.

"Everyone's worried about you," Maggie said. "You're sort of a hero now, even though we lost the game."

"They fixed your locker," Max said. He handed me a piece of pizza and a Coke. "Now it says FAG BABY TAKES A FALL, LOOKS GREAT."

"Only in one small place," Maggie said, taking careful bites, but still managing to get red sauce all over her face. It was okay; pizza is like that and it looked good on her. "Everyone hates the Tigers. If you hadn't gotten hurt, we would have won."

"Who is this everyone you keep referring to? Someone I know?" Max said.

He was already on his third piece. Maggie and I had barely finished our first. Maggie looked down at the floor. Max was making her a wreck. She was already pretty flipped about being in my room. I realize that I'm not Paul Newman, but all the same, she kept looking around at my stuff like she was in the Hall of Fame or something. If Max hadn't been there, I probably would have told her everything, all the weird stories. I mean, my room was filled with every dumb little thing I'd collected in my whole life. If Max hadn't been there, I probably would have made a fool out of myself.

Michael came in wearing his smelly carpenter's clothes, covered with a day's worth of wood shavings and sweat. I introduced him to Maggie.

"How's the leg?" he asked. "Did you take the pills?"

"They made me weird."

"That's why they're good," he said.

I wanted to tell him about how the afternoon light landed on the wooden floor, and how it felt when Mrs. Burka ran her fingers up and down my arm, but it wasn't stuff I could talk about in front of company. My mother yelled for Michael to come downstairs and he left.

"They stopped making hippies after they saw what they're like when they get old," Max said after Michael was out of the room.

"He seems to like you," Maggie said.

"Of course he likes him. Who doesn't like Jack?" Max jumped out of his chair and came running over just to pinch my cheek like he was my goddamned grandmother.

"I mean, he cares," Maggie said.

I escaped Max's pinching and nodded.

"Are they getting married?" Max demanded, sitting down and stuffing yet another piece of pizza into his mouth.

"They don't need to be married," I said.

"What about your mom?" Max asked. "Do you ever talk to her about it?"

"Not lately," I said.

There was one of those silences that pulls everyone down like a weighted fishing line. Max and Maggie looked at their sneakers and I checked out the ceiling.

"Well," Max said, crushing the empty pizza box. There were a couple of leftover pieces sitting on a paper plate. "I'll get rid of this." He collected everything and walked out of the room.

Maggie came over and sat on my bed. I felt a major hormonal power surge, which I controlled by putting my leg in the position where it hurt the most.

"I saw you fall," she said. "It was like slow motion. I could almost feel it."

"I thought you weren't going to the game."

She shrugged, and neither of us spoke.

"I like you," she said. "You're not like I thought you were."

"Thanks," I said. I couldn't say anything else.

Before, when she didn't like me, I could say pretty much anything I wanted; there wasn't a lot to lose. Now, I felt like if I said anything, it might be the wrong thing and she wouldn't like me anymore. We sat in silence.

Max came back into the room, saw Maggie on my bed, and turned red enough for all three of us.

"Am I interrupting something, or preventing a pregnancy?"

"I should go," Maggie said. "I have homework."

Max decided to be nice for once and offered to walk her home. On their way out, Maggie bent over me, and her hair fell all over my face. She swept the hair away and kissed me. It was the first time I'd been kissed by a girl who wasn't related to me. It felt good. It felt like Mrs. Burka's fingers on my arm. But it happened too quickly; I wanted her to do it again, and again, and maybe after that we could do some other stuff.

" 'Night," she said.

I could still feel the impression of her lips on mine. I wanted everything to stay right where it was for a minute so I could linger over it. A kiss. I got a kiss, I thought to myself, and started getting all happy, thinking I had a future somewhere.

Max was standing in the doorway looking all embarrassed and out-of-place.

" 'Night," I said.

"Jeez," Max said. "Is this 'The Waltons' or what?"

◇   ◇   ◇

After about four days of lying around, my leg was good enough to take back to school. The nurse's office made a whole big thing about it, and after she'd already dropped me off, my mom had to drive back from her office with a note saying that I wasn't faking it and that the school should give me an elevator key on account of its taking about three hours to walk a flight of stairs with crutches.

Elevator keys are a big deal because there's only one skinny little elevator; only teachers, cripples, and "those transporting audiovisual equipment" are authorized to use it. I finally got the key, and Max was there following me all over the place, especially into the elevator, carrying my books from class to class.

Maggie's whole bit about my nearly being a hero must have been her imagination, because no one treated me any different. Most people had never noticed I was gone. One of my teachers had nerve enough to ask what had happened to my leg and then said, "Oh, yeah, I heard we lost that game," after I told him the whole story. I felt like playing Machine-Gun Max with my crutch and punching him in the stomach or someplace worse.

Ann McCormick came up to me and pressed her face right into mine. "You lost the game for us," she whispered, not into my ear but right into my mouth. "And you didn't call me back." All afternoon I had this weird metal taste in my mouth from her braces and her breath.

Basically, everything was exactly the same as before, only my leg was trapped in a hot-dog roll and felt like something that didn't even belong to me, an independent object I was forced to carry around as a kind of punishment.

Over the weekend, my dad and Bob took me for a long ride in the country. We stopped at a pick-it-yourself apple farm. The whole thing would have been a lot of fun, except that it's impossible to pick anything when you're on crutches.

It's more like ·you've already been picked. So, I spent most of the time just sitting in the middle of a gigantic orchard. It was nice, just sitting in the grass with nothing to do. I looked at everything, taking in the size of the field, the trees, the rock wall, and the grass.

I zeroed in on the grass, and started examining individual blades really carefully, like maybe they would tell me some-thing I'd been waiting my whole life to find out. I pulled them apart. I held pieces of greenery close to my face, looking at the way each piece did in fact look quite a lot like the next. And in the end I practiced making whistles out of single blades the way my father once showed me. I tried to play the whistle, blowing and breathing, blowing into the blade of grass be-tween my two thumbs until it sang and both my father and Bob looked down from an apple tree and said something like, "Pretty good, kiddo," and I thought, Damn right.

◇　　　　　◇　　　　　◇

Monday night, I started driver's ed. Easy Method, to be sure. Michael dropped me off in front of Montgomery Ward, and I hobbled in carrying a notebook jammed up into my armpit. I was getting pretty good on the crutches, starting to check out little crutch tricks, spins on one tip and stuff like that. I took the steps two at a time, not because I was ter-rifically brave, but it was easier on account of the reach of the crutches and how you have to swing your body forward.

The classroom was in the basement, between the credit office and gift wrap. Even though it was early, the place was pretty crowded. I tried to sit down in one of those minidesks— the kind where the seat and desk are attached, but it's not a whole desk; it's more like a piece of a desk that's sort of tilted forward—so no matter what, you always have to keep one hand on the desk-top part just to hold your stuff in place.

Anyway, I tried to ease myself into the chair, and naturally it slipped away from me, scraping across the floor with a humongous farting noise.

"Sorry," I said to the gorilla face that whirled around and growled at me like a vampire on drugs.

I tried not to smile at him because I had the feeling that he was the kind of guy who'd find it offensive.

Finally, the instructor, as he liked to be called, appeared. At first, I figured that he was just another incredible nerd taking the class, but then he stepped up on the little podium at the front of the room and banged his knuckles against the side to get everyone's attention.

His pants were too short, which isn't normally the absolute worst thing, but they were plaid polyester, drip-dry gone wrong. They ended a good six inches above his ankles, showing off thick white sweat socks with red bands around the tops.

"Welcome to Easy Method," he said, pushing his greased-back hair farther back.

Everyone sat down right away and got out a pen and paper. I figured the only reason they were being so good was because they were all in a hurry to get behind the wheel. It was scary.

"Tonight, we'll begin with the rules of the road." He picked up a stack of papers and handed them to a kid in the front row. "Pass them back," he said. "I'm going to talk for forty-five minutes. Then you'll have a ten-minute break. After that, I'll continue for approximately a half hour. Tonight at the end of class, wait, and we'll sign you up for your actual hands-on driving lessons." He stopped. "You with the leg," he said, pointing at me, actually pointing. "How are you going to be able to drive?"

"It's coming off Wednesday."

"The leg or the cast," the instructor said, laughing all by himself.

I nodded. Asshole, I thought to myself. In spite of the fact that I now hated the guy, he really knew his stuff, and forty-five minutes later, I felt qualified to write traffic tickets on any highway in America.

The class broke up, and for ten minutes we were free to wander through Montgomery Ward. I hobbled along, thinking of the places where the aisles met as intersections and trying to figure out exactly who would have the right-of-way in certain situations.

Most of the kids banded together and rode the escalator upstairs to the candy department. I don't know why, but some of the crummiest stores in the world have the most fantastic candy sections. The only difference between these candy sections and a real candy store, or maybe the chocolate section in some fancy department store like Macy's in New York, is that these places sell candy that all at once is the best and the worst in the world, all in one bite, I'm not kidding. You pick out what you want, but it doesn't really matter what you get, because it all tastes the same. I go by the looks—if I like the shape, and whether or not there are any little sugar balls glued on or anything.

Anyway, you pick it out and for a dollar they give you a little waxed-paper bag filled with just enough to make you sick. The weird thing is that while you're stuffing your face it tastes great, but as soon as you've finished the whole bag, you start wishing maybe you could lie down and have someone bring you a ginger ale with crushed ice or something.

Stores like Montgomery Ward, K-Mart, and Sears also sell stuff like hot dogs that have been lying there all day, rotating around on greasy roller racks. I'm not sure why—I suspect it has to do with the way they roll over and over for ten thousand years—but these dogs taste better than anything. There's something about spinning in grease that inspires flavor.

I bought a hot dog, some chocolates, and an orange soda. Normally, I don't drink orange soda. Michael spent about an hour once telling me all about soft drinks, and most of that time was focused on orange soda, which I think used to be his favorite. According to Michael, it's not a bit orange; colorwise, flavorwise, it's all chemical. It also has a ton of caffeine in it and a preservative that, if you have asthma, can kill you. But I pretty much couldn't help myself. Montgomery Ward seemed like an orange-soda kind of a place. So I figured, go with it, and I ordered a large.

During the second half of class, we had a test. At first, I was a wreck. I'm not one of those test-taker types and I figured I'd only been in driving school for about an hour and already they expected me to take a test. It turned out to be retarded.

The questions were things like, If you are approaching an intersection and the traffic light turns yellow, do you (a) slam your foot down on the brake, throwing everyone in your car, driver included, through the windshield and into intensive care; (b) put the accelerator to the floor, giving everyone in your car major whiplash, but not quite killing them; (c) attempt to stop your vehicle without injuring anyone; (d) none of the above.

I got a 98 on the test. The only question that messed me up was something about if an animal crosses your path, do you swerve to avoid the animal even if it means putting your vehicle and other vehicles in danger, or do you strike the animal and then call the ASPCA? I got it wrong because there's no way I could hit an animal without first killing myself to avoid it.

Class ended, and I signed up for a Wednesday-evening driving lesson, thinking that my leg would've been out of the hot-dog roll for about three hours and should be pretty well recovered. As we left the room, the instructor handed us each a little book and told us to study.

"Tomorrow night, first thing, we'll have a quiz," he said, over and over again, a million times in a row, as though it were a religious thing. I figured there must be a law about how many tests you have to take before they could say you passed driver's ed.

I read the book out loud in the car on the way home, trying out the sample questions on Michael. Technically speaking, according to the Easy Method interpretation of things, Michael should never have been allowed behind the wheel of a car.

"I got my license in California. I guess things are different there," Michael said. "It wasn't all that a, b, c, none-of-the-above stuff. You explained your answers to a real-live person."

I nodded. "It's okay," I told him. I mean, after all, we both had the same answer to the animal-in-your-path question, and that was the kind of thing that counted most.

Tuesday night while I was studying three-point turns, mentally figuring which way to turn the wheel in order to get the car to go backward and to the left, I became possessed by my hormones and decided to call Maggie. I dialed her number and then hung up before the phone even started to ring. "Get a grip," I said out loud, dialing again. It's only a girl. You have to learn to get along with girls, because one day you'll marry one, I told myself. I dialed again.

"Hello," Maggie's dad said.

"Uh, hi, is—is—is Maggie there?" I would have shot myself for stuttering if only I'd had a gun.

"May I ask who's calling?"

"It's Jack." I felt like saying Mel Tillis on account of the stuttering, but I didn't know if Maggie's dad knew who Mel Tillis was.

"Oh, hi, Jack. I was talking to your father not ten minutes ago."

"That's nice," I said.

"Hang on, here she is."

Maggie picked up the phone, and even though I'd talked to her and stuff before, I was a complete wreck. Like I said before, it was hormonal or something. There were a couple of long silences, and my voice cracked everywhere. All the same, we had a pretty good conversation. We had a pretty good conversation if conversation is what you call it when you're talking to someone and you can't really think of anything to say, because all the stuff you're thinking is so pornographic that they'd probably arrest you if you said it over the phone.

"I'm glad you called," Maggie said when we were finishing our little talk.

"Yeah," I said.

Girls have the terrible habit of reducing my ability to speak to that of an infant. Mama, dada, sex, sex, is about all I can manage. I realize I'm totally socially inadequate, but hopefully it will pass. I mean, hopefully as I get older I'll be less like I am now. Hopefully, I won't grow up to be a pervert.

"So, I'll see you tomorrow," she said.

"Yeah, bye." I hung up.

My mom came upstairs. "Who were you talking to?"

"Maggie," I said.

My mom smiled. I could tell she wanted to say something about girls, or Maggie or something, but was trying to be sensitive.

"Your doctor appointment's at two," she said.

"And then I have my first driving lesson at four. Do you think my leg will be drivable?"

"We'll see." She tore a sheet of paper from my notebook and wrote one of those please-let-Jack-leave-school-early notes.

"The Easy Method guy picks me up here. You can stand in the driveway and watch me make my first three-point turn. It'll be kind of like watching me take my first steps," I said.

The next morning I was all bent over the water fountain, my busted leg thrown out to the side like a retarded giraffe's, when Max came up behind me, grabbed my neck, and pushed it down into the fountain so I was drowning, getting my hair washed, and falling all at the same time.

"Hi, guy," he said, letting go when I started coughing so hard I practically barfed. "So, listen, about this farm thing, it isn't the greatest. First off, you can't even come unless you can walk. I don't have time to carry you through fields of cow shit."

He paused for half a second and looked at me. Max had a way of looking at you that made you think he'd either never looked at you before or something drastic had happened to your face since the last time you'd seen it.

"Anyway, if you breathe in a lot of cow and horse shit,

you get a bad headache. And, my aunt and uncle run around all day arguing about strange stuff that happened like thirty years ago. I think it causes brain damage."

I stared at Max, trying to figure out how he managed those looks and how a look could cause a major crisis in confidence, like suddenly being unsure your fly is zipped or that there's no milk ring around your mouth—general stuff. I stared at Max and tried to look at him like he looked at me.

"I don't know what you're talking about," I said.

"Numb nuts, goddamned bozo, does everything have to be spelled out in forty-foot capital letters like the goddamned Hollywood sign?"

"Intimidation will get you nowhere," I said. I was drying my hair with the sleeve of my shirt.

"I'm inviting you away for the weekend."

"That was an invitation?"

"Yeah, my mother said to invite you. I told her I didn't particularly want to travel with a cripple, but she said it would be good practice for me."

Max saying his mom made him invite me threw me into one of those tailspins, the kind where you want to say yes, but you're totally freaked and the word no pops out of your mouth before you know what you're doing. All I had to do was think of the afternoon before and Max's mom and I practically had a nervous breakdown.

"I'm getting the cast off today, but I can't go," I said. "Maggie might want to do something this weekend."

Maggie might want to do something. I didn't know where the hell that came from, but it sounded good and kind of covered for my obsession with Max's mom.

"You're staying home because she *might* want to do something? You're already going out with her Friday night. What more do you want—marriage, a station wagon, kids? I can't believe you're turning down *my* mother's invitation, an invitation from a woman who likes you more than her own children."

Right there, I turned bright damn red, red like the goddamned red balloon, red like I was on the road to exploding into something I'd never been before, red on the road to purple and then blue.

"See, you admit it, but still you're turning down my invite to run around in horse shit just because some girl might, possibly, and I seriously doubt it, want to do something with you this weekend. You're nuts."

"We'll see," I said.

"We're leaving Saturday afternoon—my dad has to work in the morning. I'm telling my mother you're going."

"Not definitely." I paused. "Max, if you ever, ever tell your mother I like her, I'll kill you."

"What *are* you talking about?"

"I promise, no big thing, but you'll wake up dead one morning. I just want you to know that."

"Kind of a warning?" he said, looking totally confused.

"Yeah."

"Saturday, three o'clock, my driveway—be there," Max said.

The final bell rang and he walked off toward class.

"A farm," my mom said that afternoon on our way to the doctor's office. "My cousin Dave used to have a farm. Sheep, chickens. I loved it."

"I didn't say I was going," I said.

"It'll be good for you. The Burkas think you're great, especially Elaine—she's always talking about you."

"Maybe they'll invite you instead. They say nice things about you all the time."

"Go on," she said. "Commune with the earth."

"What?"

"Be one with the earth," my mother said.

"Mom, more and more you sound like Michael, and to be perfectly honest, it frightens me."

◇   ◇   ◇

"**H**ow you doing there, kiddo?" the leg doctor asked.

He squeezed my knee again really hard, and I started to think that maybe he had some kind of a knee fetish or something.

"Fine," I said.

"Has he been staying off it?" the doctor asked my mother. "Or have you been cheating?" he said, sticking his face right into mine.

I could see little crumbs of lunch stuck in his mustache. I made a mental note never to go to an emergency room in the middle of the night again, unless it was an emergency, like I was already dead or something.

"Jack has been wonderful, as always," my mother said.

From watching the way she kept wiggling around in her molded-plastic chair, I could tell that she wanted to kill the guy.

"Let's see what we've got." The guy wedged a pair of long, strange scissors under the cast and started cutting. It felt weird, really weird, as if my leg had been Novocained and he was cutting it off and not the cast. Finally, like cracking open an egg or an English muffin, he cracked the cast and pulled it off in one piece. "Souvenir," he said, handing it to me. Then he started twisting my leg all around, practically breaking it for real. "How's it feel?" he asked, like ten times.

I just nodded. It hurt, but not a whole lot, not like the night I fell on it. All the same, I didn't exactly want to volunteer for any additional treatments.

"Looks okay to me," he said. "I think you'll probably be able to walk again sometime soon."

"Thanks," I mumbled.

"Do some stretching exercises, like this," he said, leaning against one of the walls and doing the most pathetic stretches I'd ever seen. "Do you think you can do that?" I nodded. "Twice a day." He wrapped my leg in an Ace bandage and told me that I should keep being careful and that I could keep using the crutches part-time for another week if I felt "so inclined." I stood up and tried out my leg. It was wobbly as hell.

"Well, thanks for all your help," my mom said, collecting our stuff and practically pushing me out the door while the guy was still telling bad jokes about broken bones.

We pulled into our driveway just as the Easy Method man came to a stop in front of the house.

"Go on," my mom said when she saw me sitting in the car a lot longer than usual.

I liked the idea of driving and all, but to be honest I was a wreck when I thought about actually doing it.

"You'll be fine," she said.

And I figured sometimes mothers don't know what they're talking about. I stepped out of the car and walked across the lawn toward the yellow Chevette, toward the Easy Method man. He was standing in the street next to the car, sizing up his latest victim. I tried to walk intelligently, but my leg wouldn't really go. I ended up kind of galloping along, dragging the broken leg a little behind me, like a retarded kid playing horsey or something.

"Hi, I'm Jack," I said, sticking out my hand when I finally got to the car.

My dad always used to make me practice shaking hands and introducing myself. He'd say, "A good handshake is the key to the job market." I think it was something my grandfather used to say to him, because it made absolutely no sense.

"Vernon Walters," he said, not shaking with me. I started to walk around to the passenger's side. "Where're you going?" he asked.

"To get in," I said. "It's my first lesson."

"Driving lesson, son. You're driving."

"But I've never."

"You have to start sometime."

I galloped around to the other side, noticing a long gouge that ran the length of the car like a scar or something. I saw my mother waiting on the steps, by the front door, watching.

"Buckle up," Vernon said. "Okay. This is the ignition, this is the indicator, this is the radio—we won't be using it—this is your internal rearview mirror—adjust it so you can see through the rear window directly behind you. This is your external mirror—adjust it so you can see the edge of your car and what's behind you. How old are you, son?"

"Fifteen years, eleven months, and a week," I said.

Vernon wrote everything down on his clipboard, including the one week. "Now, adjust the seat so your legs are not cramped but so you can reach the pedals comfortably. The pedal on the right is the gas, on the left is the brake, got it?" he said. I nodded. "Don't forget it." I nodded again.

"Right gas, left brake," I said.

"Start the car," Vernon said.

He pulled out a little checklist attached to the clipboard. I felt like I was launching a space shuttle.

"Let out the clutch." I did it, remembering to give the car a little gas at the same time. "Now, down the street."

I turned the wheel slightly as the car began to roll forward. I also turned my head in about forty directions, checking for traffic around us. There was none.

My mother stood on the front porch with a bag of groceries in her hand. She stood still. I thought maybe she was holding her breath just like I was.

"You have to give it some gas, or we'll be here all night," Vernon said.

I pressed my foot down on the gas pedal. It was my bad foot; it felt hard to control. The pedal was harder to push than I had imagined. It required actual force. The car moved faster. I felt frightened, like I was on a ride in an amusement park that I'd never been in before. I didn't know what was going to happen next.

"Make a right turn up at that stop sign," Vernon said.

My head was sort of spinning; the stop sign seemed very faraway. Every two seconds, I checked all the mirrors. It made me dizzy. Vernon fed me directions like I was a blind person— left, right, look out in front, pick it up a little, don't get so close on your sides.

After about fifteen minutes, I felt okay enough to breathe. I felt okay enough to take one hand off the wheel.

"Never, ever, ever," Vernon said, "drive with less than both hands on the wheel."

I nodded and clamped down. He took me out onto the highway and made me pass a dump truck, explaining how you always pass on the left and don't cut over into the lane until you can see the other guy's headlights in your rearview mirror.

It started to get dark. Vernon told me to turn on the low fog-lights. He told me twilight was the most dangerous time of the day. He told me how the weird blue light swallows everything and no one can see anything. He told me that except for in the middle of the night, that's when all the bad accidents happen. He told me to drive home. I did, slowly and carefully.

In the end, we pulled into the driveway. Vernon had me practice backing in and out, driving in reverse, three-point turning into the street, over and over again. I could see Michael in the living room, leaning forward to watch. And even though Vernon's student-driver car was small, it felt really big and I felt lost inside it.

When the Graysons' car came down the street at the same time as I was pulling out of the driveway, I got confused, and I slammed my foot down on the brake so hard that Vernon went flying forward and it was only his seat belt that saved him.

"Do *not* allow yourself to panic," Vernon said. "Panic causes accidents. React naturally."

I nodded and pulled back into the driveway, thinking about how during dinner Mr. Grayson would probably tell Mrs. Grayson all about how the boy next door nearly killed him and that kids today shouldn't be allowed to drive until they're well into their thirties.

"Okay," Vernon said. "That ends us for today. Put the car into park, pull up the emergency brake, turn off the engine, and only then remove your safety harness."

I followed his instructions, feeling as though the roller

coaster was coming into the station and that the operator had just pressed the button that unlocks the seat bars.

"Thanks," I said. "That was fun." And before I got out of the car, Vernon signed me up for my three remaining driving sessions.

Thursday night's driver's-ed class was the one that everyone all through history talks about. It was gross-movie night. I was glad I'd already driven around a little bit, because if I'd seen the movies ahead of time, I probably would never have gotten behind the wheel.

"These are movies," the instructor said. "But they are real. The accidents you're going to see weren't staged—they happened, the people are real, the bodies are real. These movies will show you what can happen if you aren't careful, or if you are careful but the other driver isn't, or what can happen if you drink and drive, do drugs and drive, or just simply drive without your most complete attention on the road and the cars around you."

He turned out the lights, flick, flick, flick, one at a time, and started the projector. For an hour the class sat there watching movies of car accidents, of bodies being pulled out of cars, semicrushed, half-dead, moaning, crying, not talking at all, or completely dead. There was one headless body, and they showed it, showed it all.

In the beginning people gagged and said stuff about how they finally knew where McDonald's got their ground beef. People put their heads down on the little half-desks, or watched the floor instead of the screen. Some of the movies were of families showing up at emergency rooms, of police and doctors trying to figure out what had happened. They had film of people who'd survived terrible accidents, talking about the accidents, their injuries, showing scars.

In a word, it was gross. About three times, I got convinced that I'd have to leave the room. Part of me thought that if I got up and ran, the whole class would follow me. I thought we could run, through the store, to the candy section, have an orange soda, and forget the whole thing. Another part of me thought that if I ran, I would flunk the class, I would never get my license, I would never grow up, I would never be a normal human being. I stayed. I sat there, watched the movies, and felt sick.

My mother picked me up after class. "We have to stop and pick up some rug cleaner," she said. "I want to work on that spot in the hall."

She was talking about the same old Kool-Aid stain.

"Elaine told me about some new stuff that's supposed to be really good." I nodded. "How was class?" she asked. "You seem quiet. I saw you drive this afternoon. You looked good."

I shrugged. "Watch it, Mom," I said when she came within a hundred miles of another car. "Watch it, Mom," I must have said a thousand times on the way home.

When I first said it, she slammed on the brakes, and nearly got hit from the rear. "You've got to be really cautious," I said. She looked at me like maybe I had a fever or something. "Just keep an eye out, okay."

"Fine, you keep an eye out and your mouth shut unless it's a real crisis," she said.

I tried, but couldn't. I told her about the movies, I told her about checking her rearview mirrors.

"Eight seconds, check every eight seconds, that means a mirror every four seconds," I said.

"I'd have to go to a chiropractor if I turned my head every four seconds. I've been driving for a long time," she said. "I know what I'm doing."

She pulled up in front of the hardware store, and I ran in for the carpet stuff. I crossed behind a car just as it started backing out, and because I couldn't really run on account of my leg, it nearly hit me. I pounded on the trunk three times hard, and the guy was still practically running me over.

"Watch it," I yelled right into the car, even though the instructor said we shouldn't do this.

The instructor said we shouldn't yell at anyone or make certain gestures when someone does something stupid, because people carry guns in their cars and it's become popular to just point and shoot.

◇   ◇   ◇

My date with Maggie went incredibly well. If I'd known it was going to be that easy, I probably would have started dating when I was about two. I'd hung around with girls before, like when I had that thing about holding Ann McCormick's hand, but that wasn't dating.

Luckily, I didn't die of nervous collapse or hormonal overload, or say anything truly perverted or anything. I just sat there and watched a movie with her and held hands. It was all very simple. Her hand was sweaty and my hand was sweaty and the sweat just kind of mixed. Every five or ten minutes I'd pull my hand away and wipe it on the leg of my jeans to dry it and then wait a couple of minutes before I gave her my hand back.

Afterward, we went for ice cream. I kind of hobbled along and Maggie walked real slow so I didn't look like a galloping idiot.

In an effort to be, I dunno, entertaining, I ended up confessing everything. I told her about basketball and how I pretend I'm Magic Johnson, and how in my head, I hear the crowd and can feel the other guys on the team, surrounding me, protecting me while I go in for the drive. I told her all about the movies, and how I sometimes think my life is like a big movie that just hasn't been edited for television yet.

"What's your favorite film?" she asked me.

I gave her the cookie that came with my ice cream. She crunched down on it, and little crumbs fell out all over the place.

"It's not the greatest, technically," I said, "but I love *Shoot the Moon*."

"I saw that. The piano music keeps playing over and over, repeating but never finishing."

"It's great because everyone in it is right," I said, like Siskel and Ebert combined. "There's no way to take sides. Even in the end, when the father smashes up the tennis court and nearly runs the mother's boyfriend over. It all makes sense."

I stopped only because Michael once told me the best way to make friends is to let people talk about themselves.

"What's your favorite?" I asked Maggie.

"You're gonna laugh," she said, laughing.

"I promise I won't."

"I can't remember the name of it. But, it was the first movie I ever saw. Jay North, the guy who used to be Dennis the Menace, is in it. And there's this zebra who ends up in the kitchen."

"Sounds great," I said, laughing.

"I said it was stupid," she said.

I walked Maggie home, and we sat down on the front steps for a while, talking. I could hear her father and John arguing in the house. It sounded as if they hated each other.

I imagined what dating was supposed to be like: You bring the girl home and her mother and father are sitting in the living room reading *Life* magazine together and they both look up and say, Hi, kids, did you have fun? and the boy goes, Yes, Mrs. So-and-So, it was very nice. And then he turns to the girl and waves good-bye and says, See you in school.

"Not much longer before his bags are packed," Maggie said.

It was depressing as hell. We were quiet for a while. I felt like having a conversation about our fathers, you know, what it means to have a gay dad and what you're supposed to do with that information and all, but it was our first date, my first real date ever, and I didn't want to completely ruin it by getting serious.

Just before I left, she leaned toward me and, even though it was pitch-dark, tried to look into my eyes. I thought maybe she was going to kiss me. I wanted her to, but couldn't ask. I wanted to kiss her, but couldn't figure out how to do it by myself.

"You know," she said, "I used to think you were really . . ." I almost had a heart attack while I was waiting. "I dunno, kind of a jerk or something."

My eyebrows must have jumped about two feet or something. A kiss was out of the question. "But you're not." She laughed.

I smiled involuntarily. "Thanks," I said.

I felt nauseous from a combination of the ice cream and a ride on the roller coaster of love, or sex, or whatever the hell you want to call it.

"No, really, Jack, you're sweet."

"Listen," I said. "Would you like to come over one night for dinner? I'm a good cook—well, pretty good."

"I usually have a lot of homework."

"Bring it over. I'll help you."

"You, help me. You're on the verge of flunking out."

"It's not because I'm stupid. I just get distracted. You know, helping so many people with their homework that I don't take the time to do my own."

"We'll see."

"Please. Tuesday night."

"I have to be home by eight-thirty."

"Come at five."

"Five-thirty. I have dance class in the afternoon."

"Five-thirty. I don't care. Just come over." I stood up to leave. "What kind of food do you like?"

"French."

"I only know how to make chicken."

"They have chicken in France."

"Okay," I said, walking across the yard. "French chicken." I walked across the yard doing a really spastic walk, flapping my arms, my legs, everything. "Oh, oh, sorry," I said. "That's the funky chicken."

Maggie seemed to like the fact that I was willing to completely humiliate myself in front of her, and to be honest I liked it, too.

"Bye, Jack. Thanks a lot." She yelled when I was all the way across the yard, "I had fun."

"So did I," I yelled back.

"What," she screamed. I could tell she was laughing. "I didn't hear you."

"What," I yelled back as I walked down the sidewalk.

"I can't hear you," she shouted when I was all the way down the street.

"Never mind," I yelled back.

An old man inside one of the houses turned on his porch light, opened the door, and told me to stop disturbing the peace.

◇   ◇   ◇

"**M**ake sure you take your wool shirt," my mother said Saturday morning as I was trying to get my stuff together. "And extra socks."

"What are you, Max's mother?"

"No, yours. Do you think you should take your crutches, just in case your leg hurts?"

"Mom, it's West Virginia, a farm. If I get tired, I'll sit down."

"Make sure you get the phone number from Max. I want to know where you are."

"They may not have a phone."

"Jack," she said, imitating my voice perfectly, too perfectly. "It's a farm, not another planet."

I called Max to get the phone number. "Do you have any gum?" Max asked. "Sometimes, I get kind of nauseous when we ride in the car for a while."

"I'll get some," I said, imagining Max throwing up all over me. I picked up my duffel and carried it downstairs. "Ready!" I yelled out the kitchen door to my mother, who was fooling around in the garden.

I stuck the phone number of the farm on the fridge and put three packs of gum into my pocket.

"Do you need any money?" she asked.

"I have some.

She kissed me good-bye, and I went out to Michael's car.

"I lived on a farm," Michael said as he backed out of the driveway. "A commune. We grew all our own food."

He drove like an old man, bent forward, like Mr. Magoo, with one toe pressed on the accelerator so we went maybe three miles an hour.

"It was like one big vegetable garden."

Sometimes, I wondered if Michael's brain wasn't like a big vegetable garden.

"I guess I'm really a city kid," I said.

"No such thing. We all come from the land."

Michael pulled up into Max's driveway. Mr. Burka was just getting out of his car. He turned around and looked at us, then walked away toward the front door.

"Nice guy, real friendly." Michael waved at the back of his suit. "Have fun, Jackie. Maybe pick a carrot or something for me, okay?"

"No problem."

Max's mom opened the front door before I even knocked.

"How are you, Jack. Come in. Are you all ready to go? That's a nice jacket you're wearing. Do you remember where you got it? Max," she yelled, "Jack's here."

"Thanks for inviting me. I've never been to a real farm before."

Max came downstairs and herded me off to his room. "I'm working on something," he said, pushing me up the steps.

Max's Junior Scientist Chemistry Experimenter Kit was spread out all over his room. "What do you think?" he said, pointing at a paper plate sitting in the middle of his desk. Centered on the white plate were two red Twinkies. "Incredible, am I right? I wrote the Twinkie people this morning. This could be the start of a major revolution. I mean, I know they've got pink and yellow Snowballs, but never has anything edible had color so good."

I shrugged.

"Color is in, Jack. Take a bite," he said, pushing the fire engine red sponge cake toward my mouth.

"No, thanks," I said.

"Come on. Don't be a fag baby."

I shook my head. Charming, truly charming—why do the things you hate the most, things like nicknames, last forever? I pictured Max at my fiftieth birthday party making a speech about his old buddy, his pal, fag baby.

"Okay, then watch." Max bit into the cake and then pulled it away from his mouth and showed me the center. It was turquoise blue, maybe navy blue. The white cream filling of the Twinkie was goddamned blue.

"Unbelievable," I said.

"Max," his mother yelled up the stairs. "I don't want you filling up on junk food. You'll throw up in the car."

"How'd you do it?"

"Injection. It's perfectly safe, food coloring. You have to do the blue part first. Otherwise, the colors run."

"Max," his mother yelled. "Downstairs."

I followed Max down and into the kitchen. Mr. Burka was sitting at the table eating a sandwich the size of a Hawaiian island. "How's things," he said between bites.

"Good." I knew he was sort of asking about my dad, but I really didn't want to get into it on account of we were supposed to be going on a pleasure trip and all.

"Jack, are you hungry?" Mrs. Burka said. "Don't let Max frighten you with his Frankenstein imitation."

"I ate at home."

"Are you sure?" She pulled a gallon of Tropicana from the fridge and poured herself a glass.

"Are you going to calm down or what?" Max asked his mother. "I hate it when you get like this."

"Like what. Get like what?" she said.

"Okay, let's go," Mr. Burka said, jumping up from the table, practically throwing his plate at Mrs. B., who stuffed in into the dishwasher. "No delays, right now, hut two."

Sammy walked out the door carrying three stuffed animals.

"Do you have to take all that shit?" Mr. Burka asked him.

The car glided out of the driveway. As soon as we were on the road, Mrs. Burka started talking a hundred miles an hour to Mr. Burka, who pretended to be concentrating on driving. Sammy sang songs to himself. Max turned away from everyone and stared out the window. After a while, I slouched down and fell asleep.

"Watch where you walk," Max said as we wandered through the barn. It was too late.

"Wait," I said, scraping my dirty sneaker on a bale of hay. I smelled like a zoo. I had to breathe with my mouth open to keep from choking to death.

We walked around, staring at the cows and watching the sun drop slowly behind the hills. Max waded into the brook and tried to catch a fish, bare-handed. After he fell in twice and got thoroughly soaked, we headed back toward the house.

"I was just getting ready to ring the bell for you boys," Max's aunt Verna said. We took off our shoes in the "mud" room. Clearly, "mud" was another name for what I'd stepped in.

"If this isn't the life," Max's father said over and over again during dinner, between helpings. "Mountains, animals, fresh air."

"It's work," Max's uncle said. "There's nothing here that doesn't need to be taken care of."

"How do you take care of a mountain?" Sammy asked.

"Shhh," his mother said. Mrs. Burka leaned over Sammy's plate and cut his food into small pieces.

"A mountain is just a big rock," Max said. "You don't really take care of it."

"Do rocks grow?" Sammy asked.

I saw Mrs. Burka smile, but I was the only one who laughed out loud.

"Only in your head," Max said.

"Eat," Aunt Verna said, heaping more food onto our plates.

It's peculiar how people who live only a couple hours away can seem so totally different. I mean, Max's aunt and uncle were country, like the people Abe Lincoln grew up with or something.

After dinner, we all went into the living room and sat there. Just sat there. Sammy sprawled out on the floor and started drawing in and out of the lines in his coloring book. He was the only one who seemed comfortable.

"We're going to need some juice in the morning," Max's aunt said. His uncle nodded. "And some bread."

"Guess we should take a ride into town," Uncle Henry finally said.

"Can we come?" Max asked before he even finished his sentence. Uncle Henry nodded.

"Run upstairs and get your jackets," Max's aunt said. We both flew up to the guest room.

"Is it always like this?" I asked Max as I rummaged through my clothes for my red wool shirt.

"It gets worse. That's why I made you come."

"Thanks," I said, pulling the shirt over my head.

Max bounced up and down on each of the beds. "That one's yours," he said, throwing my bag off one bed and onto the other.

"I should have brought a book."

"Climb in," Max's uncle said as he started the red truck. The engine growled and groaned, before falling into a steady rattle.

"Can we ride in the back?" Max asked.

His uncle nodded. Max and I climbed up over the rear bumper and into the back of the truck.

As I sat down, Uncle Henry put the truck into gear and it jerked forward. My head banged against the glass of the cab.

"Isn't this great?" Max asked as we bounced down the gravel road toward town.

Every other minute, we'd be thrown up a couple of inches in the air and fall back onto our tailbones. By the time we got to the 7–Eleven, I was covered with gravel dust, and my butt was so sore I couldn't walk straight.

"Why don't we get a couple of these?" Max said, picking up a bunch of porno magazines from behind their YOU MUST BE EIGHTEEN OR OVER racks. "Then we'll have something to do."

"You boys see something?" the man behind the counter asked.

Max put the magazines back. I picked up a couple of comic books, a deck of cards, and a lollipop for Sammy. On my way to the register, I saw a package of metal jacks with two little red rubber balls, and remembered my mother talking about when she was little and sat on the floor of her parents' bathroom playing for hours on end. I pulled a package off the rack.

"Jacks are really queer," Max said.

"They're for my mom."

"She's like forty," Max said, as though that meant something.

I thought about Mrs. B. and wondered what she was like

when she was a kid. I wondered what she was like when she was my age, and it made me nervous and I didn't want to think about it anymore. I pulled another pack off the rack.

"Who's that for?" Max asked.

"Shut up," I said.

"You boys ready?" Uncle Henry said. He came around to the register carrying a gallon of OJ, a gallon of whole milk, and the kind of bread that Michael said people shouldn't eat because it was all chemicals and no fiber.

While I was paying for the jacks and stuff, I saw Max slip a Hershey bar and some Slim Jims into his pants pocket. I hoped we didn't get arrested out there in the middle of nowhere. It felt like the kind of place where they probably still hanged guys at dawn.

I had this picture of Max getting busted and telling the cops, who'd be stupid enough to believe him, that I'd done it, too, just because he didn't want to be in jail alone.

"Pretty slick," he said when we were back in the truck.

"Pretty stupid," I said, relieved that we were still free with no criminal record, at least for now.

When we got back to the house, everyone was still in the living room, sitting there as if they were paralyzed.

"Bath time," Mrs. B. said to Sammy. She collected his crayons and put them back into the box.

"Will you take a bath with me?" Sammy asked. He stared up at me from the floor.

"He pees in the tub," Max said.

"I think I'll skip it this time," I said.

Sammy looked like he might cry.

"Why don't I just help you take yours, okay?"

I leaned against the door frame and watched Mrs. Burka. She was sitting on the edge of the tub, testing the temperature of the water with her hand, moving it back and forth under the faucets to mix the hot and cold.

Sammy took off his clothes and hopped up and down, waiting for the go-ahead.

"Aren't I handsome without clothes?" he asked.

I blushed. "You're cute," I said.

"Be careful—it's slippery," Mrs. Burka said, helping Sammy into the tub.

"What's in the bag?" Sammy asked.

"Surprises," I said.

"Like what?" I pulled out the lollipop and handed it to him. He held it high above the bathwater. My leg was starting to hurt like hell from standing there. Mrs. B . took the lollipop away from Sammy and put it on the counter.

"You'll have it tomorrow," she said.

"And uh, this is for you." I handed Mrs. B. the set of jacks. "It's really dumb and I don't know if you ever played, but my mom always talks about it."

She reached up, caught me behind my neck, pulled me toward her, and kissed me on my cheek. But when she pulled me toward her, my weight all landed on my leg and it hurt so bad that I didn't notice the kiss. I pulled away only to save myself from screaming.

"I know it's kind of queer, but I figured maybe you'd get a kick out of them."

"Thank you," she said.

"What'd you get?" Sammy asked. "What'd you get?"

"Jacks. It's a game I used to play when I was a girl." She looked at Sammy. "Wash," she said. "Or you'll be in there so long you'll end up all pruney."

Sammy rubbed the soap over his body and onto his hair and then ducked under the water. And then all of a sudden, he stood up, stepped out of the tub, and tried to shake off like a dog.

"Dry me," he said.

Mrs. B. handed me the towel, and while I dried Sam she sat on the edge of the tub and talked. She talked like we weren't there. She talked like she was in a dream or something.

"In my parents' house, there was carpeting. It was considered a luxury. Now people want wood floors, but then, if you had carpet, you were rich. I sat out on the front stoop, and people always walked by and stepped on the jacks or kicked them out of place. 'These steps aren't a playground,' they used to say." Mrs. Burka went on and on until finally Sammy stopped her.

"Where are my pajamas? I can't go to bed without pajamas."

And Mrs. B. kind of snapped out of it, looked at me, smiled, and then got up to find Sammy pj's.

"What'd you do up there all night?" Max said when I caught up with him in the kitchen, preparing his ten-o'clock snack.

"Sammy took a bath."

"He must have ended up all pruney." I shrugged.

Max's aunt came into the kitchen, opened the fridge, took a glass of milk, and then turned toward us. " 'Night, boys," she said.

I looked at the clock; it was only about five past ten.

"Make sure you cut off the lights before you go to bed."

"Good-night," I said. "And thank you for having me here." She nodded and went out of the room.

Max ate his snack—a sandwich, potato chips, and two

apples—and we went back into the living room. His uncle was turning off the television and all the lights.

"You boys going to do some work tomorrow?"

"Sure," I said.

From the expression on Max's face I could tell that he was about to say something about how the concept of work didn't really appeal to him, but he managed to stop himself, and just shrugged instead.

"Get a good night's sleep or you won't be worth a bean."

"May as well go upstairs," Max said. "Unless you want to go outside and look around?"

And as though he had planned it, all of a sudden some animal out there started making weird noises.

"May as well go upstairs," I said.

"Chicken shit," Max mumbled.

As we passed his parents' room, I could hear Mr. and Mrs. Burka arguing. Max walked faster.

"I don't know why they have to do that all the time," Max said.

I shrugged. "Everyone argues. It's normal."

"You don't know what you're talking about." Max closed the door to our room. I opened the deck of cards from the 7–Eleven and shuffled them about two hundred times.

"Game?"

Max waved me away. I played solitaire. His parents were still fighting. We couldn't hear the words, but the tone came through loud and clear. Mostly, it was Mr. Burka yelling at Mrs. Burka, and every now and then she'd try to get a word in.

I looked around for a radio or a television, something to turn on. There was only a small ceiling fan. I pulled the chair away from the desk and stood up on it in order to pull the short, dangling string.

"We should get pneumonia just not to hear them?" Max said. I shrugged and went back to the cards. "Deal," he said. "Gin."

Three games later, Max quit. He crawled into his bed with the comic books I'd bought and left me playing solitaire.

I sat on the goddamned brown-and-green-plaid bedspread and looked around the room. It was decorated exactly like the Roy Rogers restaurant near my house.

"Remember when your dad and my dad took us to that ball game and we snuck off to get a hot dog and got totally lost and started crying and they had to put our names up on the scoreboard to tell our dads how to find us?"

"Yeah," I said.

"I liked that."

And Max didn't say anything else. I remembered it. I remembered that we got lost because Max had wanted another hot dog and his dad said no. We tried to be real cool about sneaking out, so we didn't look to see where the seats were, and when our dads finally came to the security office to pick us up Mr. B. was so mad he nearly killed us both; luckily my dad stopped him.

Max fell asleep, and I got my comic books back and read them each about four times before I curled up and fell asleep like a good buckaroo.

⬦   ⬦   ⬦

"Breakfast is ready," Max's aunt said when she knocked on our door. I couldn't help but notice that it was still dark outside.

"Max," I said, whispering only because that's the way you

have to talk in the dark. He didn't move. The ceiling fan was still whirring. I stood on the desk chair and turned it off.

"What're you doing?" Max asked without lifting his head.

"Breakfast's ready."

"It's the middle of the night."

His aunt knocked on the door again. "You boys up?"

"Be down in a minute," I said. Max rolled over. I pulled on my clothes, went into the bathroom, and soaked my face in ice-cold water.

"Where's Max?" Mr. Burka asked when I sat down at the table.

"You look very healthy," Mrs. Burka said.

"Is he still in bed?" Max's dad growled.

"Getting dressed, I think." Mr. Burka jumped up from the table and charged toward the steps.

"Max," he yelled. "Get up. *Now!* Hut two."

Everyone at the table stared at each other.

"How many eggs for you, Jack?" Aunt Verna asked, breaking the stare. "Three?"

"Two, please." She slid the sunny-side ups off the platter and onto my plate.

"Potatoes?" I nodded. She heaped them onto the plate.

There was a stack of toast the size of the Empire State Building sitting in the middle of the table. I took a slice and used it to mop up the egg yoke.

"Max," Mr. Burka yelled again. "If I have to come up there . . ."

"Stop it," Mrs. Burka said. "This is a family, not the army."

"Shut up, Elaine," Mr. Burka said, and then he slammed out the kitchen door and into the front yard. Max slowly came down the stairs.

"What's the deal?"

"He's just in a mood," Aunt Verna said, handing him a plate with four eggs and about five pounds of potatoes.

Max sat down and ate. His mother poured him a glass of orange juice and then refilled it again when it was empty.

"You boys gonna work this morning or what?" Uncle Henry asked.

"I can't milk a cow again—I just can't. The cow nearly committed suicide before I finished last time."

"No, we've got to clean out the pool. It shouldn't be too hard, for two boys."

"Where's the pool?" I asked.

"Right out there." Uncle Henry pointed past the sliding doors in the living room. "We put it in a couple of years ago."

"I like to swim," Aunt Verna said.

"Please, can I have some more?" Sammy said.

Everyone turned toward him. He was holding up his plate like Oliver Twist.

"Oatmeal?" Aunt Verna said.

Sammy nodded.

"Anyone else?" she asked. We all made faces.

"I'll get it," Mrs. Burka said, picking up Sammy's bowl.

While she was in the kitchen, she opened the door and said something to Mr. Burka, who was still walking circles in the front yard. Eventually, he came back in, sat down at the table, and we finished breakfast without anyone saying a single word.

"There's just a few frogs and some eggs," Uncle Henry said. He handed me a long metal pole with a net on the end. "Drop everything into the bucket."

He gave Max a rusty metal bucket that looked more like

a giant trash pail than a bucket. "If you need me, I'll be in the barn," he said.

Max walked toward the swimming pool, and I hobbled along behind him. To be honest, my leg wasn't quite ready for farm life. Walking on a sidewalk is one thing, but farms are bumpy as hell and that's not something you can explain to a busted ankle.

Max and I walked across the yard. There was fog everywhere. I couldn't even see the barn, or the driveway, or anything except the ground under me.

"It's seven-fifteen," Max said, pushing the button on his digital watch. It beeped back at him.

The grass was long and dewy. After about three minutes, our sneakers were sopping and made sucking noises as we walked.

"I don't like to be up this early," he said. "Especially on a weekend. It's emotionally dangerous."

I lifted the latch on the pool gate.

"I get crabby," Max said.

He flipped over the bucket, put it down on the cement deck, and sat on it. I walked to the edge of the pool. The water was clogged with millions of clear things, like jelly, like marbles, clinging together like bunches of grapes.

"There's probably medical literature, hard facts about how bad it is to eat breakfast before daylight," he said.

Some of the additional half million brown things floating on the pool—brown things that I first thought were leaves— started to move, and I realized they were frogs.

"Max," I said. "There's something here."

He came over to the edge of the pool, took a quick look, and then turned around and threw up behind a bush.

"Are you okay?"

"Barely," he said.

I dipped my net into the water and filled it with the jelly marbles—frogs' eggs.

Max wiped his mouth across his sleeve, spit into the grass, and flipped the bucket over so I could dump the net in.

Even in the dull premorning light, the eggs glistened like some weird new-wave jewelry.

"You sure you're all right?"

"Fine, fine." Max looked as green as the grass. "There's nothing like breakfast at seven, frogs at seven-thirty. Yep," he said, taking a deep breath and jutting out his chest. "It's the life."

I dropped another netfull into the bucket. Two small brown frogs fell out as I flipped the net. Max chased them across the yard. With his bare hands he scooped both of them up and tossed the little critters back into the pail.

The whole thing became kind of an acrobatic routine. I'd run the net through the water, scraping up whatever I could, and then, with water dripping everywhere, I'd swing the net toward Max, who very quickly lifted the top off the pail and helped to dump the net, using his body to block the escaping frogs.

By the time the fog completely burned off, I had a thick line of sweat across my top lip and my leg was throbbing.

"What are you doing?" Sammy yelled across the backyard. "Can I go swimming?"

Max shook his head, and I dropped another batch of frogs into the bucket.

"This isn't a regular swimming pool," I told Sammy, who stood pressed against the metal gate, waiting to be let in.

"It's a dinner pool," Max said. "Uncle Henry keeps live things in here and then takes them out when he's hungry. We're fishing for tonight's dinner, go away."

"What's in there?" he said, pointing at the net, almost completely filled with little brown frogs.

"Frogs," Max said, lifting one out and throwing it at Sammy, who first burst into tears and screamed hysterically and then almost as quickly began laughing like a madman.

"Frogs," Max said, throwing another one at him. "Frogs, frogs, frogs, frogs," Max said, and he began pelting Sammy with the little brown jumpers.

Sammy laughed and tried to catch them in midair.

The little brownies landed on the grass and quickly hopped away as Sammy chased after them, sometimes lunging, throwing his whole body into the wet grass, hoping to catch one before it hopped again.

Finally, Max stopped throwing frogs long enough to help me finish with the pool. Together, we carried the pail of frogs and eggs back to his uncle in the barn.

"Is that really dinner?" Sammy asked, following us so closely that twice he stepped on the back of Max's shoe and I thought maybe Max would kill him.

"Yeah, it's dinner," Max said.

"I'm not eating," Sammy said. "I don't like frogs."

"How do you know?" Max said.

"I had them once at my friend's house. You weren't there." Sammy was totally lying and doing a terrible job of it.

"Well, don't tell Aunt Verna, 'cause her feelings will be hurt. She thinks frogs are your favorite—that's why she asked us to catch them."

Sammy didn't say anything.

"You wouldn't want to hurt her feelings, would you?"

"Don't worry," I told Sammy. "If you don't like 'em, I'll take yours."

He looked totally relieved. We put the pail down next to a hay bale.

"What've you got there?" Uncle Henry said, lifting the lid and looking into the pail.

"Dinner," Sammy said.

"Is that right?"

"Frogs are supposed to be my favorite food."

Uncle Henry nodded and sort of shook his head like maybe he had some water in his ear. "You can leave 'em over there," he said, pointing to a place right next to the cow's stall.

We carried the bucket over and set it down. Just as we put the pail down, the cow took one look at Max and started bellowing as though someone had tried to kill her. Sammy ran out of the barn.

"Fine job," Uncle Henry said, and then went back to trying to fix some rusty machine.

"I'm starving," Max said, once again pushing the button on his watch and causing it to beep. "It's a big ten-thirty and I'm starving to death."

We walked back toward the house, our sneakers still squeaking wet.

◇   ◇   ◇

"Go upstairs and get your things together. You all are leaving in a few minutes," Aunt Verna said as soon as we walked into the kitchen. I thought she was angry at us for coming in to get a snack before lunch. "Go on up and pack."

"I'm hungry," Max said. "We just want something to eat. No problem. I won't make a mess."

"I'll make you a sandwich. Don't be difficult, not now. Just go on and do what I say."

"What's going on?" Max asked.

I couldn't help but think that old aunt Verna was missing a few marbles.

"Sammy, run down to the barn and tell Uncle Henry to come up to the house. I need to talk to him."

Sammy slammed out of the kitchen door without even thinking of asking why.

"Where's my mother?" Max asked.

"Upstairs, getting her things together."

"And my father?" Aunt Verna shrugged. "What's happening?" Max leaned hard against the refrigerator.

I stood in the doorway thinking that I should somehow disappear.

"Your parents had a little argument, so your mother wants to leave early."

Max went flying out of the room and up the stairs. Aunt Verna opened the refrigerator and tried to act like there was nothing going on.

"What kind of sandwiches do you boys like?" I shrugged. "You'll need to eat something in that car. It's liable to be a long ride home."

She looked at me like she was pleading for me to go along with her pretending that everything was fine.

"Max likes ham-and-cheese, Sammy eats anything Oscar Mayer, and I'm not picky."

Aunt Verna pulled everything out of the fridge and started making sandwiches like she thought an army would march through at any minute.

"Jack," Max yelled down the steps. His voice was all cracky. "Come here."

"Excuse me," I said to Aunt Verna, who was spreading mayo over about a hundred pieces of bread. I ran up the steps to the Roy Rogers room. Max was piling stuff into his suitcase like a maniac.

"He hit her. There's a thing on her face that's gonna be black-and-blue in about an hour."

It was like I didn't understand what Max was saying.

"My father just beat my mom up, get it? He hauled off and slugged her like Muhammad Ali or something." Max zipped his bag. "Pack, you idiot!" he screamed at me. "We're leaving."

In about two seconds, I scooped all my stuff together and stuffed it back into my duffel bag. Max sat down on the bed and started crying, but then stopped himself.

"What an asshole," he said. "It's not the first time, you know."

I tried to be cool; Max wouldn't even look at me. In some weird way I felt guilty, as though I was the one who'd hit his mom. I didn't know what to do. The family that I'd always thought was perfect, better than my own, was suddenly crumbling and taking my best friends with it.

"I have to get Sammy," Max said, jumping up and running out of the room.

I closed the door and sat back down on the bed, trying to imagine Mr. Burka—the Cub-Scout leader, the baseball fan, the complete heterosexual—slugging Mrs. Burka, the lady with sexy hands, who used to play jacks on the front stoop. I tried to imagine him hitting her not once, but on what seemed like a semiregular basis. It didn't work. I didn't believe it. It made no sense.

I thought Max was exaggerating. I figured his parents had an argument like one my parents had a long time ago.

My mom was sitting at the kitchen table, reading the paper and eating a chocolate doughnut. My dad came in and they started fighting about something stupid. I saw my dad pick up the box of chocolate doughnuts and throw them right at my mom. She just sat there, frozen. There was chocolate all over her face and a little paper cut on her cheek from where the box had hit. After a second, she started crying and my dad was apologizing all over the place.

Someone knocked on the door and I snapped out of my trance. Mrs. Burka walked in, sat down on Max's bed, picked up his pillow, and hugged it to her. It was nothing like when my dad threw the doughnuts. The whole right side of her face was a kind of purplish red and puffy, like raw meat or eggplant, plus there was a little bit of dried blood in the corner of her mouth. I tried to not look at her, but couldn't help but look. I looked and I burst into tears and started wailing like an idiot.

It was strange because it wasn't my mother, and it wasn't my father, but it seemed like it was. It was as though everything that had happened to my family and everything that I'd ever felt about the Burkas or anyone had welled up inside me and was spilling out all over the place.

After a while, I slowed down enough to go over to Max's bed and sit down next to his mom. I hugged her and then started crying a whole lot again, and she started crying, too, and then Max and Sammy came upstairs. Sammy was already crying when he came into the room, probably because Max was practically yanking his arm off.

We all huddled together, pressed close, like an Oreo, crying and kind of chanting. Max was saying, "He's such an asshole," over and over again. Sammy said, "Mommy, Mommy, Mommy." Mrs. Burka just kind of went, "Ahh, wahhha," and I felt as though at any second I would start screaming and never stop.

Aunt Verna came into the room and directed everyone. "Hush, hush," she said, then disappeared and then came back with a wet washcloth, which she pressed against Mrs. Burka's forehead. "Hush," she said again, and again, until eventually we all stopped crying out loud. Aunt Verna pulled a handkerchief out from somewhere inside her sleeve and handed it to Max's mom.

I ran into the bathroom and brought back a whole roll of toilet paper. We sat there crying and trying not to cry, blowing our noses and rubbing our eyes until we all looked red and raw.

Max and I threw the suitcases into the car and went back into the kitchen. Mrs. Burka was sitting there with an ice pack pressed to her face, watching Aunt Verna pack food into two big bags as though we were preparing to cross the Mojave Desert.

I kept thinking that Mr. Burka might show up. I mean, not being too familiar with wife-beating protocol and everything, I was pretty confused. I kept trying to plan what to do if he came back angry. I remembered there was a fireplace poker in the living room; I figured if I had to, I could grab it and swing at him while Mrs. B. snuck out.

"Take care of your mother," Aunt Verna said to Max, pulling him slightly aside as the rest of us walked to the car.

I was looking forward to being in the car where it was safe, where we could lock the doors.

"Make sure you call me as soon as you get home," she said. "Or if you stop along the way, use a pay phone, call collect, let me know what's going on. Maybe I should come with you. Should I?"

Anyone could tell Aunt Verna was flipping out and in no position to come along for the ride. Uncle Henry walked up from the barn and toward the car. "I'd better stay for Henry," she said, and we all nodded.

Uncle Henry just looked at Mrs. Burka and then started hugging her. He hid his face in her shoulder and held on for the longest time before opening the car door and letting us in.

"He's my brother," Henry said, after Max's mom started the car. "But I feel like killing him."

Mrs. B. put the car in gear. I immediately locked all the doors, and we started creeping out of the driveway. I felt sort of bad for not saying, Thank you for having me, to Max's aunt and uncle, but the timing wasn't right.

As we moved down the gravel driveway, past the barn and all the small outbuildings, we started going faster and faster. Mrs. Burka was speeding down the gravel road and everything started to disappear in a cloud of gray dust. I got scared that maybe she was on a suicide mission or something. But, as soon as we hit the real road and were away from the farm, she slowed down and I realized that she just needed to get the hell out of there.

No one talked. The car bounced up and down the hills. On either side we were surrounded by farms, just like the one we had left so quickly. Max pulled sandwich after sandwich from the bags Aunt Verna had packed, and stuffed them into his mouth, one after another, occasionally offering one of us a half.

I had part of a chicken on wheat and half a PB-and-J on the kind of bread that's whiter than white and tastes like stale cotton candy.

I kept trying to imagine Mr. Burka hitting Mrs. Burka.

Every time I got close to the moment where something bad happened, my mind froze. Then, I imagined myself bigger, older, busting in on the Burkas just as he was about to hit her. With one arm, I blocked his punch; with my other I made a fist and knocked him one against the jaw. I saw Mrs. Burka and me, the two of us looking down at Mr. Burka passed out on the floor. I promised her it would never happen again.

Right then in the car, I felt as bad as I'd ever felt, totally powerless, like a child. I wanted to do something for Mrs. B., to protect her. I wanted to do something for her as nice as the afternoon she had tickled my arm. I wanted to marry her.

"I'm not going to let anyone kill me," Mrs. Burka announced as we rolled down the highway.

I was glad she was taking a stand.

"Don't let him," I said. It was the equivalent of saying amen, only not at all religious.

Her voice cracked all over the place just like my dad's did when he took me out on the lake, only this time there were no big confessions to come. Max swallowed his sandwich and burped. Sammy lay in the way back of the station wagon, pretending to sleep.

After a while, Mrs. Burka turned on the radio and started singing along with the old Stevie Wonder song, "You Are the Sunshine of My Life." She sang with a warbly voice like a demented bird.

The weirdest thing was how Mrs. Burka knew the words to almost every song. I couldn't help but think she spent a lot of time driving around in the car, singing at the top of her lungs, especially because Max and Sammy didn't seem the least bit fazed.

As we went down some of the hills, the radio got staticky and faded out, but Mrs. Burka kept singing. She had a good voice once she got going, kind of Joni Mitchellish, only with a little more bite. If the radio faded and she couldn't remember the words, she made up new ones, sometimes a whole new tune. Sammy started joining in, making up choruses, and at one point even Mighty Max added a few verses of his own.

We passed signs I hadn't noticed on the way to the farm— huge paintings of Indians riding horses and carrying bows and arrows. FRONTIER TOWN 2.5 MILES ON RIGHT, the next sign said. There was a picture of some Indians dancing around a fire.

"Are we stopping?" Max asked.

"We always stop at Frontier Town," Sammy told me, like it was something from a fact file I'd forgotten to read.

"Aren't you getting a little bit old for cowboys and Indians?" Mrs. Burka asked.

Parents always think their kids are getting too old for stuff, but as far as I'm concerned no one's too old for anything.

"I want a tommy gun," Sammy said. "Daddy said I could get one, he promised."

"Tomahawk, idiot," Max said. "And Dad's promises don't count."

"Let's make this a quick one, okay?" Mrs. Burka said as she pulled off the highway and into a gravel parking lot.

Frontier Town wasn't exactly a town; it was more like an aluminum warehouse with a lot of oversize wooden cutouts of Indians glued onto the front.

Mrs. Burka turned off the car and reached for her wallet. She handed Max a twenty. "Buy Sammy what he wants."

"Aren't you coming in?" Max asked.

She adjusted the rearview mirror so she could see her face. It looked pretty bad, as though someone had hit her with a baseball bat or something. She shook her head.

"Go on without me."

Max and Sammy poured out of the car and stood waiting for me.

"I think I'll stay," I said.

I had this image of myself as a grown-up, sitting in the car, talking to her while the kids were in the store. I imagined her telling me all kinds of things that she'd never told anyone before.

Max shrugged like he thought I was crazy only didn't want to mention it. He grabbed Sammy's hand, and together they walked across the gravel parking lot toward the big chief hanging over the entrance.

"Don't stay because you feel sorry for me," Mrs. Burka said, watching me in the rearview mirror.

I looked back at her incomplete reflection in the small rectangular glass. Staring at the purple around her eye for too long, I noticed how the color faded from a beefy meat red around the outside edge to a soft velvety violet and then darkened through a hot plum that looked the most painful, and into a midnight-blue purple, like a starless August sky. She looked away.

"I don't know what to say," I said.

"You don't have to say anything," she said.

Don't say anything, she said, just as I was about to say, I love you.

It was the only thing I could think of that meant anything. I shifted in the backseat, first slouching down and then sitting up very straight.

There was a pay phone next to two Coke machines on the far side of the parking lot, and I realized I should probably call my mom and tell her that I'd be back early.

"Be back in a minute," I said, opening the door and getting out.

"I'm sorry," Mrs. Burka said, apologizing without even knowing exactly what she was apologizing for.

"I just have to call home."

I walked away from the car, scraping my sneakers through the gravel, kicking up some smoke. Pulling the phone booth shut, I dialed 0 and then our number. The operator came on.

"Collect to anyone from Jack," I said, and in the background I heard the phone ringing and ringing.

"I'm sorry. No one answers."

"Could you please try 555–8302."

There was a pause and then I heard two rings, a pickup, and Bob's voice.

"I have a collect call to anyone from Jack. Will you accept the charges?" There was a silence, like maybe old Bob had to stop and think about it for a minute. Finally, he said, "Um, yeah."

"Hi," I said. "Is my dad there?"

"Hold on. Telephone!" Bob yelled, and my dad picked up the other extension.

"Hello."

"Dad," I said. "Dad."

"Is everything okay, Jack?"

"I'm coming home early. We went to the Burkas' farm." The connection was lousy.

"You don't sound good."

"Mr. Burka hit Mrs. Burka."

"What do you mean, hit her?"

"Slugged her, you know with his fist, like boxing."

"Where are you?"

"At a phone booth in front of Frontier Town. I called Mom, but no one's home."

"Is Elaine okay?"

"I don't know," I whined. "Her face is like mincemeat, and Mr. Burka disappeared. It was horrible."

My voice started shaking. My dad didn't talk. I kind of cried a little bit, but felt like a fool. I mean, I was standing in a phone booth, in front of Frontier Town, staring at god-damned wooden cutouts of Pocahontas and her crew.

"Jack, how far from home are you?"

"I don't know, maybe an hour." I looked through the dirty glass of the booth at the blue edge of the mountains, which now seemed faraway. "We should be home soon."

"I'll meet you at the Burkas', okay? Just hang together until then." I nodded, but obviously he couldn't see me. "Jack?"

"At the Burkas'," I said. "You'll pick me up."

"Yeah."

"You promise you'll be there."

"Of course. Don't worry—everything will be fine. I'll see you in a little bit," he said, and then hung up.

The phone made a few *beep, blip, beep* noises and then went dead. I pulled the phone-booth door open, glanced across the parking lot at the station wagon, and then walked in the direction of the big chief over Frontier Town's front door.

Inside, there were rows and rows of stuff—war toys, as Michael would say—painted in bright colors: tomahawks, spears, headdresses with ten colors of feathers, including hot pink and lime green. There were three-cornered hats like the ones the old guys from Williamsburg wore; and plastic bubbles with scenes of cowboys and Indians fighting, filled with water and little white snowflakes that float around when you shake the bubble.

"Pick one thing," I heard Max tell Sammy from all the way across the store.

I passed a bin that was filled with incredibly old dirt-covered dented bullets that a sign claimed were from the Civil War. I picked out two.

"I thought you wanted a tomahawk," Max said. "That's a spear."

"I don't care," Sammy said.

"What are you getting?" Max demanded as soon as I caught up with them. I showed him the bullets. "Big deal," he said, flashing his find at me. It was a long silver knife with leather wrapped around the handle. I stepped backward as he pointed it at my stomach.

"What the hell are you buying that for?"

"It's a throwing knife," he said.

I felt like telling Max how warped it is to throw knives, but I let it slide.

"See my tom-a-spear," Sammy said, waving a long wooden pole with a bunch of colored feathers and a rubber spearhead attached to the end back and forth in front of my face. It looked like a prop from a school play. Near the cash register, there were cases filled with arrowheads, fossils, and stones. I picked out a bunch of stuff, including a nice piece of turquoise I figured my dad might like. My whole family liked little stones and stuff you can keep in your pocket, to play with when you're flipping out. The salesclerk, dressed like a squaw, wrapped everything up in old newspaper and dropped it into an official Frontier Town paper bag.

"Did you get what you wanted?" Mrs. Burka asked when we got back into the car. It was obvious that she'd been crying.

"I got a spear instead of a tommy hawk," Sammy said, showing his mother the painted wooden pole.

"The feathers are very pretty," she said, starting the car and easing it out of the lot and onto the highway.

"What'd you get?" Mrs. Burka asked Max.

"Just some thing," he said, pulling the change from the twenty out of his pocket and dropping it onto the front seat.

"I got these," I said, showing her the old bullets and rocks. She held on to the hunk of turquoise so tightly that I couldn't ask her to give it back. I felt guilty. I couldn't imagine why I hadn't thought of buying her a present. "You can have it if you want," I said, and she smiled, then handed the rock back to me.

The radio played, but no one sang. Max sat in the back, behind his mother, so she couldn't see him rubbing his fingers back and forth across the thick blade of his knife, until finally his skin gave out and his fingers bled.

He looked at me, like he wanted to check and make sure that I was watching, and then wiped the blood on the thighs of his jeans, wrapped the knife up, and put it back into the bag.

My father was sitting on the Burkas' front steps when we pulled into the driveway. He walked so slowly over to the car that by the time he got there, Max, Sammy, and I were already out and our suitcases were lying on the asphalt.

"Hi," he said, to all of us, avoiding Mrs. Burka. When he finally looked right at her, I thought he might start crying;

his face got all screwed up like a bulldog's, but then he looked down at the ground for a couple of seconds until it dissolved back to its normal position. "I'm sorry," he said to Max's mother, looking at her again. "I'm so sorry."

Mrs. Burka raised up her hand toward her eye, like she was going to block it off so no one would have to see, but then instead her hand kind of swept past her face and reached out to my dad. He put his arm around her shoulders, and they started walking toward the house.

"How come he's here?" Max asked.

"Because I called him," I said, sitting down on the bumper of the car, totally relieved that at least now someone was in charge.

"What do you mean, you called him?"

"From the phone booth at Frontier Town."

Sammy picked up his bag and started walking toward the backyard.

"Where are you going?" Max yelled at him.

Sammy reached up, unlatched the gate, and pulled his suitcase through the dirt toward the playhouse in the backyard.

"Sammy," I said, walking fast to catch up with him. "I'll come with you, okay? Can I?"

Sammy nodded. Just then, my mom's car pulled into the driveway, nearly running over my duffel bag.

"What'd you do, send smoke signals?" Max shouted at me.

My mother ignored us and went marching up to the front door, like maybe she expected to find Mr. Burka in there waving around a goddamned machine gun or something.

I turned around and followed Sammy. On my hands and knees I crawled into the fake log cabin that Max and I used to play in when we were kids. Sammy was still short enough to stand up inside.

"I'm scared," he said, looking out the glassless window at the back of his parents' house. "I'm scared," he said again, louder, like he thought I didn't hear him the first time.

"I am, too." He looked at me as if I'd turned from a boy into an elephant and back again. "Everybody is." I held Sam tight against my chest. And then I felt bad about being so honest on account of how Sammy was just a kid. "It'll be all right."

"Where's my dad?" he asked.

"At Uncle Henry and Aunt Verna's."

"When's he coming home?"

"I don't know." Sammy pulled away and sat on the floor of the cabin.

I stretched my legs out in front of me. They nearly touched the opposite wall. On summer nights when I was little, sometimes Max and I would plan to spend the night in the cabin. We'd unroll our sleeping bags, lie on the dirt floor, and make up horror stories until we finally got each other so scared that we'd go running back into the Burkas' house and hide out in the kitchen eating cookies until Mrs. Burka would say something about how we should probably give up on the idea of camping out on account of it being either too hot, cold, or rainy outside. Max and I would grumble for a while, and she would try to make us feel better by saying we could play camp-out in the den with the TV on.

"Are my mom and dad divorced?" Sammy asked.

"No," I said, and thought of my own parents, together for the first time in a long time, inside the Burkas' house.

"Maybe we should go inside?" I said.

Sammy shook his head. And as curious as I was about what was going on in the house, I couldn't leave Sammy. We sat together in silence on the dirt floor of the moldy old cabin.

"We're getting pizza," Max said, leaning in the window that was more like a hole cut into the cabin than any window I'd ever seen. "What do you want on it?"

"Meatballs," Sammy said, crossing his arms in front of his chest and glaring at Max, waiting for him to say no.

"Who's going?" I asked.

"Your dad."

"Where's my mom?" I asked.

"Upstairs, in my mother's room."

"And my dad?" I asked. I knew they were somewhere in the house, but I needed to know where, in what proximity.

"I told you, going to get pizza. What is this, a quiz show?"

I walked out of the cabin, leaving Max and Sammy, and went into the Burkas'. My father was sitting at their kitchen table, doodling on a memo pad. "Gonna have some pizza?" I shrugged. "You know, your mother's here."

"I saw her drive up."

He nodded. "Mrs. Burka's friend Rosalie is up there, too."

"Anyone hear from Mr. Burka?" I asked.

"Nope."

There were footsteps on the stairs, and we were quiet. My mom came into the kitchen. I think seeing my dad sitting there talking to me freaked her a little bit, or maybe she was already that way.

She pulled a cigarette out of her pocket and motioned for me to come over to her. I did, and she looked at me like I was two years old and then started playing with the hair behind my ears while she smoked.

"This is bad, isn't it," I said, even though it was obvious.

Her fingers were tickling the hell out of me, but I couldn't move. They both nodded.

"Max and Sammy are flaking out," I said.

My voice cracked and my mother pulled me closer and hugged me and I started crying. I don't usually cry. My dad got up from the table, came over, and hugged both of us. We were all pressed together like an ice-cream sandwich, and both my parents kept saying, "I'm sorry," over and over again.

Max and Sammy came into the kitchen, and we separated, moving back into our corners like boxers. My dad sat back down at the table. I stood in the middle of the room, and my mom leaned against the door and lit up another cigarette.

"Where's Mommy?" Sammy asked.

"Upstairs," my dad said.

Max sat down at the table, picked up the pen that my dad had been using, and finished my dad's doodles on the same piece of paper.

"So what about this pizza thing?" he said.

"Let's order," my dad said, dialing the phone and handing it to Max. "Get two with whatever you want."

"Guess I should go back upstairs," my mom said, stubbing out her cigarette and then, I think only because Max was a witness, dumping her whole horrible collection of butts into the trashcan and rinsing out the ashtray. Normally, she lets them collect for like a week.

"Get some beer when you pick up the pizza. Okay?" she said.

I looked at my father. He was on the verge of saying, Since when do you drink beer? but stopped himself by staring down at the worn-out place on his loafers. As my mom drifted out of the room and toward the stairs, I had the strange sensation that it was a long time ago, and we were still all together the way we used to be.

"You gonna come for the ride?" my dad asked Max and me.

"I'm too young to buy beer," Max said. He concentrated on doodling.

"You sure?" I said.

He shook his head. "Traveled enough for a day. To hell and back," he mumbled.

"I'll go," I said.

◇   ◇   ◇

"Sammy asked me if his parents were divorced," I told my dad as we drove to the pizza place.

He kind of grunted, "Ummm," and ground the gears when he shifted.

"Do you think they will? I mean, so suddenly. Is it over?"

"Things go on for a long time, and no one ever knows. You find out about something, and it seems sudden, but it really isn't."

I thought of him packing all his stuff into the giant green trashbags and thought about saying, Like when you left, but didn't.

"It's not the first time he hit her. Did you know that?" He shrugged like he didn't want to say. "Did you?"

"A long, long time ago, the Burkas had a fight, Elaine ended up with a broken arm, and Sandy left for a few weeks."

I had a vague memory of something once happening and my dad taking Max's mom to the emergency room while my mom stayed and took care of me, Max, and Sammy, who was a baby.

"Did you take her to the hospital?"

He nodded. Somehow, I thought she had tripped on the stairs or over a toy or something.

"Why didn't you do something?"

"Like what?" he said.

"Stop him."

"Jack, it's not that easy. I hardly talk to Sandy anymore. I didn't know anything was going on."

My father shifted the gears again, the car made a horrible, painful sound, and I thought about the fact that in a month I'd be getting my learner's permit and would probably have to practice my three-point turns in the same blue Volvo that had haunted my childhood.

He pulled into the pizza place's parking lot and almost clipped the front end of a Camaro that was pulling out.

"Be careful," I snapped.

My father ignored me and parked the car. The pizzas weren't quite ready, so we sat in a booth and waited.

"Your mom looks good," my dad said as he played with the cheese and hot-pepper shakers.

I wanted him to say more. I wanted to ask what he really thought. Did he notice that her hair was longer than ever and sort of gray in places? Did she seem too thin to him, smoking too much?

"She seems happy."

"She is," I said, very definitely. I always felt obligated to defend my mother, even when she wasn't being attacked.

"That's good," he said, putting the shakers back down on the table with a loud bang.

He looked right at me, wanting something I didn't have, and then all around the restaurant.

"I went out with Maggie Friday night," I said.

"Really?" He sounded sort of surprised, and I couldn't tell if he was faking it or not.

"Yeah, didn't you know?" He shook his head.

"It was good. I mean, I had fun."

He nodded and smiled one of those really thin, internal smiles that people do by accident when you say something that reminds them of something that happened to them like three hundred years ago.

"She's coming for dinner Tuesday night. I'm cooking."

"Soon, you'll be borrowing the car and I'll be up all night wondering where you are."

"Guess so," I said, even though it seemed unlikely that he would even know when I was out. Then there was one of those killer silences that weighs a ton. We both looked at the floor pretty seriously, like it was our job to count the number of tiles or something.

"Your birthday's in a couple of weeks."

"I know," I said. "Three more Easy Methods and I'm through."

"You're growing up."

"Guess so."

"You're growing up, and I'm getting old."

I didn't answer. I mean, what was there to say.

"Bob's gonna be fifty soon. Does he seem old?"

"I dunno," I said. My dad looked down at his knees. "He doesn't look fifty, if that helps."

He raised his shoulders and then lowered them. His jacket stayed up in the air with empty shoulders.

The pizza guy finally called our number, and as we went up to the counter, my dad stopped at the cooler, pushed back the cold glass doors, pulled out a six-pack of Molson's, and handed it to me. Then, he reached back in and got a six of Coke.

"I'm going to stay here tonight," my mom said when we were cleaning up the stuff from dinner. Mrs. Burka, Sammy, and Max were upstairs getting Sam ready for bed.

"I'll take Jack back to the house," my dad said.

"Thanks."

My mom smiled at my dad like she'd met him for the first time fifteen minutes ago. She dropped her cigarette butt into a beer bottle and swished it around in the spit at the bottom.

"Tell Michael I'll call him in a little bit," she said, hugging me. "See you in the morning."

" 'Night," I said.

And then, as we started for the door, my mom hugged my dad and they held on to each other for a while.

"Let's talk sometime," my dad said, pulling away from her.

"Soon," she said.

Max came downstairs and pulled me out the front door toward my father's car. "You're not going to tell anyone about my mom, are you?" he asked.

"No," I said.

"I mean, I did tell a couple of people about your dad, but that was different."

"I'm not planning on having a press conference," I said. "But it's not different. Private is private."

Max shrugged. "Yeah, well, I guess I might have made a mistake, or something."

"Guess so," I said.

"But, you won't tell?"

I shook my head.

My dad came out to the car. "Ready?" he asked. I nodded.

"Max, take care," he said, putting his hands on Max's shoulders and kind of hugging him a little bit. Max wasn't an easy kid to hug.

"Bye," Max said. My dad ground the old blue into gear, and we drove off down the road.

"I can't go right home," he said as we got closer to our house. "I'm not ready yet. Do you want an ice-cream cone or something?"

"I'd probably throw up."

"How about a walk?"

"My leg isn't exactly itself." He made a left onto my street. "I might be able to shoot a couple of baskets or something," I said.

"Thanks."

He parked in front of the house and waited while I ran in to get the ball and to tell Michael that my mom was staying at the Burkas'. When I came back out, he was leaning against the car. "The park?" I nodded.

"Should we walk or ride?"

"I can probably walk okay," I said.

It was a nice as hell night, and what's a little pain? Compared to everything else, my leg was nothing. We went down the street bouncing the ball between us. At first, I couldn't really see what I was doing, but then my radar kicked in. I could tell exactly where the ball was without ever seeing it. I just knew, just like that, I knew.

I went down the sidewalk ahead of my father, my leg dragging a little bit, but not too much. I walked ahead of him dribbling the ball low, close to the ground. It was getting cool, and I could feel the little hairs on my arms standing up. We walked in silence, but it was as though we were talking. We were silent, but we were talking more and better than we had in a long time. I passed the ball to my father; he took it into the street, dancing in and out of the parked cars.

Right near the park, we passed a small pond, the same pond where we used to ice-skate in the winter. We passed it, and I could see a reflection of the moon on the water. There was a thin breeze, like before rain, and the reflection moved back and forth in the rippled water. I thought of the lake my father took me to when he told me he was gay. I thought of the lake and I looked up at the white moon. I looked across the dark street at my father. He passed me the ball. Without even seeing it in the air, I caught it. I caught the ball and I thought about the lake, about the dragonfly hovering in the air above the scum. I thought about what my father had told me. I thought about it and it didn't matter anymore.

The courts were empty and the lights were on, bright. They were the same kind of lights television crews use to film in the dark. "Magic Johnson," I yelled, going in for a lay-up. It was slow, my leg didn't feel like it was my own. The shot missed. My father took the rebound off the board and put it up again, through the net. I grabbed it and dribbled. I went in for my most famous shot, my turnaround jumper, off the backboard and through the net. The nets in that park are the best in the world. They're metal and make a smooth swishing noise when the ball goes through. But always, just before the ball drops, it hovers there for a second, trapped by the metal.

I got hot from the lights, from trying to run back and forth on the leg that wasn't made for stops and starts. My shirt stuck to my back. Every breath went into my throat like a sip of cold water. My dad was running hard, weaving in and out, dodging imaginary men. The glow of the lights made me feel like a star. In my head I imagined the rest of a team there with me. In my head I heard the roar of a crowd. Each shot I took counted for something more than two points.

After about forty-five minutes, my dad took a shot from just under half-court. He hurled the ball toward the basket. It fell through the net without ever touching the sides. My dad collapsed onto the court half-laughing, half-crying. The ball hit the concrete, bounced a few times, and rolled to a stop.

I lay down next to my father. I could feel my pulse beating in my leg, throbbing. I could see our hearts beating through our shirts. I looked at him, at the sweat moving down the side of his face, curving into thin lines between his whiskers. He closed his eyes and smiled.

"This is it, Jackie," he said. I didn't answer, because there was nothing to say. "This is where I always want to be."

We lay there for a long time until my shirt dried, stiff, as though it had been hanging on a line for a week. We lay there until our sweat turned cold and we had to walk just to keep from freezing.

◇   ◇   ◇

"I take it you're no farmboy," Maggie said when she caught up with me at my locker just before lunch.

I threw my books into the bottom, closed the door, and looked at all the fag-baby stuff written on the outside. I figured at the end of the year, they'd probably charge me for it.

"I asked Max if you guys had a fun weekend, and he looked at me like I'd just escaped from Terminal Island, or had a peanut-butter sandwich stuck in my braces, and I don't even have braces."

I thought of Ann McCormick and her braces and felt like a jerk. She'd probably grow up to be the first woman president, and in her inauguration speech she'd say something about how she always had nice hands but it didn't matter because all people ever noticed were her braces.

"It was a long weekend," I said to Maggie.

"Did something happen?" I shrugged. "You don't want to talk about it?" I nodded. "Do I have ESP or what? It's okay. If you don't want to talk, then just say so."

"I just can't talk, not right now."

"Are we still having dinner tomorrow night?"

"Max has nothing to do with dinner," I said. "But—" I paused. "Look, can we postpone it? Things have gotten very complicated—and it's all too horrible." I took a breath. "I really need to spend some time by myself."

"Yeah, sure, okay."

"It has nothing to do with you, I promise."

We walked to the cafeteria in silence. I liked that about Maggie. I liked how I could be quiet with her and she didn't hold it against me.

A lot of people get flipped out if you're quiet. They say stuff like, What are you thinking? And if they don't start interrogating you, they start talking, going on and on about stuff that's totally irrelevant, and the silence gets so big and loud that it's scary.

Max came over to the table when Maggie got up to get an ice-cream sandwich.

"Thanks a lot, shithead," he said, picking my hamburger up from my tray, taking a couple of bites, and then dropping it so it fell into the little puddle of applesauce. "I thought you weren't going to discuss my mother's face with anyone, and then, first thing I know, before I'm even together about it,

Maggie comes up and says, 'So, did you guys have fun?' If I wasn't the guy I am, I would have decked her right then and there. I would have decked her on the spot."

Max took the french fries from my tray, swept them through the ketchup, and stuffed them all into his mouth. He chewed with everything showing.

"I didn't tell her," I said. "I didn't even see Maggie until a couple of minutes ago, and she told me that you goddamned growled at her this morning."

I looked across the cafeteria and saw Maggie coming through the ice-cream line.

"In fact, Max, I've been avoiding her all day because I don't want to talk, not about your mom, not about anything. I feel like nothing makes sense anymore. Okay?"

Maggie caught my eye and then, when she saw Max standing there, made a face and sat down at a far table with a bunch of girls.

"Are you going to finish this?" Max asked. He stuck his index finger into the applesauce and then popped the finger into his mouth.

I pushed my tray over to him. He ate everything, including the part of the hamburger roll that had been soaking in applesauce. In fact, he used the goddamned burger roll as a kind of scoop for the "chilled fruit dessert," on account of my having forgotten to pick up a "silverware packet," as they liked to call it.

During Spanish class, which for me was right after lunch, someone knocked on the door. "Enter," Mrs. Mason said in Spanish. We all watched the door. In most schools people don't go around knocking on doors, unless it's the principal's office. Usually, you either walk right in or you don't bother at all. "Enter," she shouted in Spanish. Mrs. Mason had a short temper with no logic at all. The door still stayed closed. She slammed her chalk down into the little chalk holder that ran the length of the blackboard. It split in half; then both pieces fell to the floor and broke again. "Come in already," she said, storming over to the door and yanking it open. "What do you want?" she said to the wheezy guy standing out in the hall. Whoever it was, he was the kind of guy who considered office duty a kind of business course; maybe he was preparing for a future as a vice principal or something.

"I didn't want to interrupt," he said. Half the class started laughing. The kid turned bright red, almost heart-attack purple. He handed Mrs. Mason a slip of paper and disappeared. She looked down at the paper and then walked over to my desk and handed it to me. The whole class memorized her moves like maybe there'd be a test on it. How many steps did it take me to walk to Jack's desk—in Spanish, of course. Nine. *Nueve.* The paper said that my father had called and I was supposed to call him back. "Go," Mrs. Mason said. I shrugged, meaning that it could wait. "Go now," she said. And while everyone watched, I wiggled out of my desk. It was the retarded kind of desk; one piece, with all the wrong measurements between the desk and the chair. I escaped and ran down four flights of steps to the pay phone that was hidden away between some lockers and a girls' bathroom.

"Jack," my dad said in a real calm voice, like he was in the middle of a goddamned golf course.

"What's wrong?" I said.

"I just wanted to see how you're doing."

"At school?"

He didn't answer. I poked my fingers into the coin return. It was empty.

"I talked to your mom this morning. She said that Elaine

isn't going to let Max's dad come back. Apparently he wants to, but she won't let him into the house."

I rubbed my sneaker across the metal floor of the phone booth, across the raised silver diamonds. It wasn't something I wanted to talk about from a phone booth in the lobby of my school.

"Is it as simple as all that—one minute you're married and the next you're not?" I asked.

My father didn't say anything for a couple of minutes, and then, as though it was a social call, he started talking in a whole new tone of voice.

"Your birthday's coming up. We should plan to do something nice. Sixteen doesn't happen every day."

"Dad, I'm at school. You're calling me at school. It's not normal to call a kid at school. Sometimes kids call their parents, but parents don't call their children. They just don't."

"I was worried about you, that's all. This Burka thing is very hard." I nodded, even though he couldn't see me. "I love you," my dad said. Someone rapped hard on the glass.

"Why aren't you in class?" It was the hall monitor.

"Family emergency. I'm talking to my father."

"Hurry up," the hall monitor said. I closed the door.

"Look, Dad . . ."

"Jack, I feel terrible about this whole thing. I mean, I feel terrible about everything, about how I left when I left and all of it. It probably wasn't done the right way." He stopped.

"There's not a right way," I said. "Look, I've got to go. Just try to calm down a little or something. It'll be okay."

"Are you sure?" he asked.

"Yeah, I'm sure," I said, wondering why all of a sudden I sounded like him and he sounded like me.

"Well, good," he said. "Look, Jack, the other thing is that

Bob and I are having a cocktail party tonight, a fund-raiser for this woman who's running for Congress, and I wanted you and Max and Maggie to come."

"We don't vote."

"You'll have fun."

"You want Max at your house for a party?"

"He could stand to be out of Elaine's hair. Mom will bring the two of you over after your driving lesson—it's all set. See you later," he said, and hung up before I could say anything, like No, or I have other plans, or anything.

◇　　　　◇　　　　◇

"**D**id you ever notice how you can drive right up into the sky?" I said to Vernon while we were out brushing up on my driving style.

"Son, keep your mind on the road," he said.

I was driving out River Road. The sky was a million colors. It was the color of bruises without the green parts. I could still see the bottom half of the sun, but everything else was purple and pink and hot red. Don't think I wasn't concentrating on driving—I was—but there was no way not to notice this stuff.

When I went up the big hill, I had this strange feeling that if I kept going, if I drove as fast as I could, there was a chance that I would get right up there with the sun and I thought for a minute that maybe I could drive straight through it.

"Slow down," Vernon said. "Don't go running away with your foot on the pedal." On our way back to my house, we went by the Burkas'. It wasn't something I planned. In fact, it was Vernon's idea. I don't mean that passing the Burkas' house was his idea, but practicing on the side streets was, and he kept telling me to make this left and that right and finally there I was cruising past their house. Mrs. Burka's car was in the driveway, and so was Mr. Burka's, and there was a car from the county.

I knew it was a county car, because it said so on the side. It had a little map of where we live, and it said FOR OFFICIAL USE ONLY. I don't know why they bother putting that official-use stuff on the outside. It doesn't really mean anything to anyone who's not driving the car. It should be on the inside so that the people in there know what they're supposed to be doing. I dunno. It's all very confusing.

Anyway, I saw the cars there, and the whole thing made me nervous as hell. I saw Mr. Burka's car and my mind started racing. I thought that maybe he had come back and that he and Mrs. B. had fought again. I thought maybe something worse had happened. I thought all about stuff like that, about parents being together and then one leaving. I thought about all that while I was driving, and Vernon started yelling at me because I wasn't paying attention to what I was doing and the car kept drifting all the hell over the place.

Vernon wanted me to keep driving for a while, to practice in the dark, but I told him my stomach hurt. I told him that I felt sick and might throw up in the car. I told him that, and he told me to go ahead and drive home.

"Mom, Mr. Burka is over at the Burkas' house and there's an official county car there, too," I said as soon as I walked in the door.

I shouted it because I thought she was probably in the kitchen or upstairs or something, but it turned out she was right there in the living room all bent over the Kool-Aid stain, trying to get it out with the stuff Mrs. B. had said we should use.

"Sandy went to pick up some of his things, and Elaine's lawyer said it would be better if someone from the county or the sheriff's department was there, too, just to keep things straight."

"You mean that was a cop car? Mr. Burka's going to jail or something?"

"He's not under arrest."

"Assault. That's what Bob told Dad it was."

"I know what it's called, Jack. I watched 'Dragnet' when I was growing up." She stopped. "It's a messy situation."

"She's not going to have Max's dad locked up, is she?"

"I don't think so, not if Sandy stays away from them."

I sat down on the sofa and watched my mom scrub the stain for a while. Michael could probably have done a better job on it, but he refused to be involved on account of how he thinks the fumes from household-cleaning products, rug cleaner included, cause about 30 percent of all cancer.

"How was your day?" she asked me. I shrugged.

That was what she always used to ask my dad when he came home from work. But, I didn't have a day—I only had school.

"Did Max seem all right? You should try to be nice to him now."

"I am nice," I said. And it was pretty much true, or at least I thought it was. "Aren't I?"

"Of course you're nice. I only meant that he needs you now."

Wonderful, I thought. He needs me. "Dad called me at school today, to sort of check on me." She laughed. "It's not funny."

"He really is a good guy," she said.

"It was embarrassing as hell."

She laughed again and then tried to stop herself. "How was driving?"

"Fine," I said.

"The very first day I had my license I crashed into a police car. I just backed right into it. Dented the fender a little, but it broke the taillight on my Aunt Sally's Chevy."

"Did you get a ticket?"

"No one saw me, so I drove away."

"You wrecked a police car and then just drove away. They're probably still looking for you."

"Shhh," she said. She stopped scrubbing the carpet. "Your birthday's coming up pretty fast."

"I know."

I was a little annoyed. I mean, how could I forget, even if I wanted to: It was x-ed out on the calendar with red Magic Marker.

"We should do something nice. I was thinking I'd like to have a little party, a dinner party."

Birthday parties make me nervous as hell. They're one of those things where you're forced to be happy. And even if you're totally depressed, you've got to pretend you're glad you were born, regardless of the fact that getting older means you're getting closer to dying.

"I was thinking I could invite your father, Bob, Elaine, Max, Sammy, and Maggie, if it's okay with you?"

"It's kind of short notice?" She didn't answer. "It might make everyone uncomfortable. Dad and Bob haven't exactly been hanging out here or anything."

Seeing my dad and mom together for things like busting my leg and Mrs. Burka getting beaten up was one thing; they were what you could call emergency situations. But the idea of my dad, Mom, Michael, Bob, and everyone else sitting at our dining-room table—well, that was something I needed one of my mom's Valiums just to think about.

"I could make roast beef. Bob's not a vegetarian, is he?"

I shook my head.

"Do you want me to ask your father or do you want to? Jack, you're growing up. We all have to grow up, don't we?"

"I'll ask him tonight when I'm over there," I said, already rehearsing a way to phrase it so my dad could chicken out without feeling bad.

She smiled. "I'll bake a cake," she said. "Call Max, invite them for your birthday, and tell him we'll pick him up in twenty minutes."

I dialed Max's number. "Do you realize," Max said, "that from now on your birthday will coincide with the date that my mother forced my father out of our house and wrecked our family. From now on," he said, "your birthday will be like the anniversary of the Holocaust for me."

I didn't know what to say. I didn't feel like I could tell Max everything would be okay. I couldn't tell him he shouldn't be angry.

"I think it's important for us to be together," I said, and it came out sounding a lot more like my mother than I ever thought I was capable of. It came out like proof that I was aging fast.

"We'll be there," Max said. "And then when you get your license, you have to promise to get me the hell out of here."

"I'll take you for a ride."

"I don't mean a ride, I mean out of here, like to California or something."

"We'll be there in twenty minutes," I said.

"Now that's what I call service."

◇ ◇ ◇

"This is where he lives?" my mom said as we drove up to my dad's apartment. "It's so, so indistinct. How do you know which one is his?"

"You go by the numbers," I said.

"He can certainly afford to live better than this," she said, and then she got quiet, I think because she felt like a jerk for saying nasty things right when they were starting to be friends again and on account of Max and everything.

"Call me when you're done and I'll pick you up," she said. We climbed out of the car. "Try not to make it late—it's a school night."

"See you later."

"Have fun," she said.

She sat there in the car, and I thought maybe I should invite her in or something.

"Let's go," Max said, pulling at my sleeve, and finally my mom started to drive away.

You could hear the noise from my dad's apartment as soon as you got to the second floor. It started as a kind of gentle hum, like a vacuum cleaner. As we climbed the steps, the sound got louder and louder so that by the time we got to the door, it sounded like people were yelling inside. I rang the bell five times, and no one answered, so Max went ahead and opened the door.

There were like thirty million men and women crammed into my dad's apartment. I recognized a couple of my dad's old friends, guys who used to hang out at our house on

Saturdays and sometimes spend the night on the living-room sofa and wake me up early on Sunday to play basketball. I pushed through the crowd with Max holding on to my belt loop, which annoyed the hell out of me because I kept thinking it looked queer and I didn't want anyone thinking anything. My dad was in the kitchen, alone, attacking a giant blob of ice with an ice pick.

"Hi," he said, hitting the ice pick with a hammer. "Did you see Maggie? She's here with her dad."

"We just walked in," Max said. "Where's the food?"

"In the living room."

"Is everyone here gay?" he asked, looking out into the living room. My dad laughed. I didn't think it was funny; I was thinking exactly the same thing.

"No," he said.

"How do you know who's who?" Max asked.

"You don't," he said.

Max leaned out the kitchen door and looked around at the people in the living room. "I guess it's safe enough," he said, and headed off toward the food.

I leaned back against a cabinet. Every time my dad hammered the ice, the back of my head banged against the wood. In about two seconds I had a headache.

"You want me to put out the ice?"

He handed me the bucket. I worked my way across the living room, looking for Maggie. Her father's boyfriend stopped me just as I was putting the ice down.

"Oh, thank you," he said. "Did you bring that out just for me?" He reached into the bucket while I was still holding it and practically knocked it out of my hands. "My little Maggie's around here somewhere," he said, and then gave me a horrible smile, as if to say, How cute, heterosexual children—what will they think of next. I hated him.

Some lady came up to me and said, "You must be Jack—you look just like your father. Is your friend Max here? How's school? I hear so much about you."

She was talking to me as though she knew me, and it made me nervous as hell on account of how I'd never seen her before in my life.

I saw Maggie across the room and she saw me and we motioned in the direction of the front door and it turned into a kind of race to see who got there first.

"Get me out of here," Maggie said when I met her at the door.

"Let's go." I opened the front door, we ran down the length of the hall, and then all the way down five flights of steps.

We sat down under a pine tree, the only tree in front of the building.

"I hate your father's boyfriend. I absolutely hate him."

Maggie started laughing. "He eats his toenails. He clips them off and then puts the pieces in his mouth."

"Totally gross," I said, even though I ate my fingernails—well, not exactly ate them, but when I bit them off, I chewed up whatever I got.

"I love my dad," Maggie said, as though when I said that I hated his boyfriend I implied that I also hated him. I didn't know what to say. I mean, if I said, I love your dad too, it would have sounded really queer.

"Don't you wish your dad would find some girl and get married?"

"No," Maggie said, quickly, like she hadn't thought about it or maybe she'd thought about it for a million years and the answer was already there, just like that. "I'd be totally jealous."

We were quiet for a couple of minutes. I didn't know what to say.

"I love my dad, too," I finally said.

Maggie jumped up and grabbed my hand. "Where's Max? Didn't he come with you?" She pulled me up off the ground.

"I left him upstairs," I said, and then at the same exact moment Maggie and I both started laughing hysterically, picturing Max trapped in the living room with Maggie's dad's boyfriend, Bob, and a hundred politically correct men and women dying to make small talk. We ran back into the building and up the stairs.

In the stairwell two flights down from my dad's apartment, we found Max. He was kneeling on the floor with his head stuck inside the trash chute. I tapped him on the back. He tried to lift his head up but banged it on the top of the chute.

"Are you stuck?"

"No," he said into the chute, and it echoed all the way to Africa.

All of a sudden his head went in deeper and his whole body pitched forward and he made the most revolting noise.

Maggie looked like she was going to throw up just listening to him.

"Are you going to be okay?" I asked.

Max didn't answer. I wondered why he was throwing up in the trash chute instead of in the bathroom like a normal person.

"Want some ginger ale or something?" Maggie said.

"Great. That'd be great," Max said in a really sarcastic way. "Why don't you go and get it?"

Maggie left, and Max pulled his head out of the chute. His face was pale and sweaty.

"What's wrong with you?" I asked.

"Nothing." Max pulled a bottle of vodka out of his pocket and took a big swig.

I could tell it burned the back of his throat by the expression on his face. I grabbed the bottle and dropped it down the chute.

The whole place smelled rotten—like alcohol, an old stairway, and throw-up. I propped open the door, just so I could breathe. Max started to kind of pass out or something and I got nervous as hell. I could see the headline: TEENAGER DIES AT HOMOSEXUAL COCKTAIL PARTY.

Maggie came back with a bottle of ginger ale and Bob.

"It was all I could find," she said, and I knew she was talking about Bob and not the ginger ale.

"Come on, Max," Bob said, picking Max up all by himself.

We tried to sneak Max back into the apartment, but everyone saw him and kept asking, "What happened?"

My dad came running into the bedroom with a doctor friend of his, and they propped Max up on the bed and covered him with towels in case his cookies came up again. The doctor took Max's pulse and watched him breathe and pretty much decided he wasn't about to die or anything.

"I hate to call Elaine," my dad said. "She doesn't need this."

He picked up the phone and called my mom. They started talking about Max and Mrs. B. and we were all standing around watching him talk. Then the conversation got weird and he was talking about my mom and himself, and everyone was still standing there, incredibly out-of-place, and I felt more out of it than anyone because it was my mom and my dad and my Max.

"We should leave," Bob finally said, and we all filed out of the room in a long, thin line.

Somehow it got decided that Max and I should spend the night at my dad's and deal with the rest of it later.

Before Maggie went home, we had a whole long talk about our fathers and I told her all about Max's mom and dad so she'd know why Max'd become an alcoholic and stuff. When she left, I kept wishing I could go with her.

"See you tomorrow," she said, waving good-bye. And tomorrow felt like it would never get there.

Bob and my dad set up the sofa in the living room, and we walked Max out there and tucked him on one side.

"You're a good boy," my dad said, kissing me on the forehead. I was nearly sixteen and he was talking to me like I was a three-year-old.

"You're a good man," I said, kind of patting him on the back. He didn't get that it was a joke or anything.

" 'Night," Bob said.

" 'Night," I said.

And Bob and my dad walked down the hall and closed the door to their room.

I was lying there, with Max in an alcoholic stupor, snoring next to me, and all of a sudden I was incredibly lost. The lights from outside made little designs on the carpet and it was like the world outside was a million miles away. I was alone, totally alone. I wanted to run down the hall and get my dad, but he was with Bob and I didn't know what they might be doing. He was a stranger—everyone was. I felt like crying, but didn't because it would have woken someone up. I just lay and lay there until finally I fell asleep.

$\diamond$ $\diamond$ $\diamond$

The day before my birthday, I woke up with a tingling sensation in the part of your stomach that's just below your stomach itself but still attached to everything. I woke up with the feeling that big things were going to happen soon. I woke up remembering the dream I was having just before my eyes opened.

I was grown-up, maybe twenty-five, driving a red convertible down the street toward my house. The street was a lot like the street I live on now, only I knew it wasn't the same street. And in the dream, as I was driving, I was thinking about the garden at my house and that I should plant tomatoes.

When I got out of bed, I kept thinking about the dream, not what I dreamed, but how I appeared in the dream. I was taller, and my shoulders had spread out. My hair was shorter, parted on the side.

I checked in the bathroom mirror. There was no part in my hair; it just kind of fell all over the place. I tried to comb a part in, but it didn't stay. I stuck my head into the sink, soaked my head, scraped a comb along my scalp, and forced a part in.

At school, I had a day-before-your-birthday kind of day. The kind where you walk around in a daze trying to figure out your whole life, because in less than twenty-four hours, it won't be the same anymore.

The fact is, when you turn sixteen, you're not fifteen anymore. There's no escaping the fact that you're getting older, that you probably have all the hair under your arms you're ever gonna get, and so on. I went around obsessing about whether or not I seemed like sixteen and came to the conclusion that in some ways I'm about sixteen, seventeen, or eighteen, but I'm also a lot like a twelve-year-old.

What I'm trying to say is that my idea of a good time is the same now as it was when I was a kid, only it's getting tougher to pull off. And while I was thinking all this stuff, I had the overlapping thought that now more than ever, I'm stuck between things. I'm stuck between being a kid and being an adult. The things that kids do aren't really a whole lot of fun, but what adults do still seems too hard, and to be honest, boring as hell.

I was telling myself all this terrible stuff in the middle of history class, in the middle of a movie on Reconstruction. I told myself that it didn't matter about being stuck. I told myself that the line between being an adult and being a child was a small one and that I knew a lot of adults, mostly Michael's friends, who acted like retarded kids.

When I got home, there was a message from Vernon on my mom's answering machine, saying that he'd be about an hour and a half late because some kid smashed up his car and he had to get the door banged out enough so it would open and close before we could have our final go-round.

I went outside, picked up my b-ball, and started off down the street. I'd planned to go to the park, but about halfway there my leg started hurting and I headed for the playground at my old elementary school.

It was on a hill above the school. There were fences everywhere, so when the little kids, who couldn't aim, threw a ball, they didn't have to run down the hill and into the street to get it. Generally, people are pretty good about doing things like that to keep little kids from getting run over and stuff.

I stood there on the hill, looking down into my old school. There were still classes going on because it was only about three o'clock, and even though we get out at two-thirty, the little kids don't get out till three-thirty. It's because they start later and not like they're being tortured or anything. Every couple of minutes, in the classroom nearest me a million little hands all of a sudden shot up into the air, and then slowly, one by one, came back down.

I dropped the b-ball and it rolled across the dirt, stopping at a rusty swing set that probably should have been condemned. Even though I shouldn't have, on account of my leg, I climbed to the top of the jungle gym. I thought of hooking my knees over the bar and hanging upside down like I used to do when I was a kid. But when I looked down, I saw that if I tried, I'd probably get a concussion or something. I mean, the jungle gym was only about three feet off the ground. I got down.

In the dirt near my ball I found a fake diamond ring. It was the kind of thing you get from the dentist's office when you let them clean your teeth and don't bite the doctor or anything. I put it in my pocket.

The basketball hoops for elementary-school kids are about eight feet tall. I guess they make them short to give the kids hope. If the hoops were regulation, no third or fourth grader would ever score. They'd probably get totally depressed and quit basketball forever.

Personally, though, it was confusing. My radar was tuned for ten feet. So, at first, I kept automatically aiming for a regulation hoop. The ball kept going up and over the whole damned backboard. Once I figured things out, I realized that for the first—and last—time ever, I could slam-dunk as well as any guy.

"Fast Jack takes the pass from Smith," the announcer's voice boomed in my head. I ran unevenly across court, wondering if and when my leg would be completely working again. "Fast Jack is coming in low and fast," the announcer said. I crouched down, dancing in and out, avoiding my enemies. My leg felt like I was stepping on pushpins, again and again. "He's up," the announcer said. "Fast Jack puts another one through for two." I shot a few more, and in my head I could hear the crowd screaming, and the announcer talking about my averages, and so on.

But before I heard him say the game was over, I had to stop. I was turning into a cripple. My busted leg was dragging behind me, like it was dead. It felt like if I took one more shot, if I jumped up one more time, I'd end up back at the doctor's office, and this time he'd probably amputate from the knee.

"Jack, is that you?" my mom said when I walked in. She came out of the living room with a rag and big bottle of Glass Plus. "Are you sure your leg is healed enough to play ball?" she said when she saw the ball tucked under my arm.

"I'm not playing," I said. "Just bringing it in from outside." I didn't want to get into it.

"I found some new stuff to try on the Kool-Aid stain," she said. "It's supposed to be industrial strength."

"Great." I mean, what can you say about carpet cleaner. I went upstairs, dropped the ball on my floor, and took three aspirins.

Vernon beeped when he pulled into the driveway. I grabbed a jacket and went out to his car. The whole driver's side was bashed in. In fact, the part that used to say EASY METHOD DRIVING SCHOOL had completely disappeared.

"You've got to lift the door a little in order to open it," Vernon said when I tried to get in. I pulled on the door, and it finally opened with a ripping sound, metal against metal.

"Guess you don't want to talk about it, huh?" I said. He

shook his head. I backed out of the driveway and cruised down the street.

"Let's take it slow," Vernon said. Eventually, he cooled out enough to let me try out the beltway. He suggested I practice passing trucks. "You've done well," he said an hour and a half later when I drove up in front of my house.

From under the pile of papers on his clipboard, he pulled out a certificate that said I'd passed driver's ed. It was all filled out and everything, so obviously Vern knew ahead of time that I was on my way.

"Thanks," I said, trying to open the door.

"Good luck, son," Vernon said.

And as much as I wanted to get out of the car, I couldn't because the goddamned door wouldn't open. In the end Vernon had to get out, come around to my side, and practically rip the car apart to let me out.

"Thanks," I said.

"Good luck, son," Vernon said again, as though it was in the rule book that *Good luck, son,* was the last thing you were allowed to say to an Easy Method graduate.

◇   ◇   ◇

On the morning of my birthday, my mother tiptoed into my room and whispered, "Are you up? I want to show you something. It's downstairs."

I followed her downstairs, still half-asleep. I imagined that she would open the front door and my red convertible would be parked in front of the house.

"Here, kiddo," Michael would say, throwing me the keys.

"Don't look," my mother said when we got to the bottom of the steps.

"If I don't look, I can't walk," I said.

"Give me your hand," she said.

I put my hand in hers and closed my eyes. She led me.

"Okay," she said after we'd taken about ten or eleven steps. "You can open them."

I opened my eyes, and there was nothing. I mean, there was everything that had been there before, but nothing new. There was no huge box with a big card with my name written on it.

"Happy birthday," my mother said, hugging me.

"What?" I said.

She pointed down. "It's gone. The stain is gone."

I looked at the carpet, and sure enough it looked clean, so clean that it was like a reverse stain, a stain of clean on an otherwise dirty gray weave.

"Looks good," I said.

"I think I'll do the whole carpet," she said. "Not today, but maybe over the weekend." Michael came downstairs. "Stain's gone," my mother told him.

"With all the shit you put on it, I'm surprised that the whole carpet didn't disappear. Happy birthday, kiddo," he said to me.

"Thanks," I said, turning to go back upstairs and get ready for school. Stain removal wasn't exactly a red car, but I figured it was a sign of something good.

"I'll pick you up right in front of the school at two-thirty," Michael said. "We'll run over and get your learner's before anyone even knows you're sixteen."

"That'd be great, thanks."

"Should we give you a present now, or wait until tonight?" my mom asked.

"Tonight," I said.

The weird thing about having your birthday on a school day is that by the time you get to be ten, or eleven for sure, no one at school knows it's your birthday anymore. It's not like when you're little and your mom brings cupcakes for the whole class. But even though no one knows, you walk around like it's supposed to be a national holiday. You walk around thinking that people are supposed to be nice to you, like maybe on your birthday you're ten times more breakable than on any other day. Well, it doesn't work that way. It just doesn't.

First off, the school nurse saw me walking down the hall, without a cast, without crutches, and demanded the elevator key back. When I tried to explain that I still wasn't allowed to go running up and down the steps, she pulled me into her office and made me sit there while she called my mother to see if I was lying or not.

Then, when I finally got to history class, Mr. Carroll was handing out a test on Reconstruction, which I totally flunked. I have enough trouble reconstructing my life without being expected to remember how they put back together a whole goddamned part of the country. After class, Maggie cornered me in the hall, pressed me up against a locker, and kissed me like it was something she had to do to stay alive.

"Happy birthday," she said.

I moved away from the locker on account of a lock was digging into my back, threatening to sever my spinal cord and paralyze me from the waist down. The late bell rang.

"See you," she said.

"Yeah, see you," I said, distracted. Mentally, the kiss was still happening.

I went to my locker, and next to Fag Baby someone— probably Max—had written Happy Birthday. And I imagined that when I graduated, someone would write FAG BABY GROWS UP in big letters on the school roof, right next to CLASS OF 19 whatever.

I looked out the window near my locker. I looked through the metal window guards that they put up to make the place unbreakable, like a prison. It was one of those days when the sky is bluer than blue and the only clouds are about a million miles up and look just like the cotton balls we used to use for clouds in dioramas.

Even though it was totally against the rules, and in fact illegal, I went right out the front door and down the steps. It's not particularly against the rules to go out the door, even though they don't like it, but you can get arrested for leaving school property during the day. As soon as I got to the sidewalk, I started running. I started running as best I could with my leg still all imperfect. I'm sure if anyone had seen me, they would have thought I was practicing for the Special Olympics. I didn't even know where the hell I was going, but I went. I just kept running until my leg started to feel like I had stepped on a nail or a knitting needle or anything long and sharp. I cut through about fifteen backyards and finally ended up in front of a huge shopping mall near our house.

There was one of those movie theaters with about twelve things playing, twelve movies that I'd either already seen or had no desire to see. I handed the lady my money and went into the one that had just started. I stood in the back of the theater until my eyes adjusted and I could see my feet at the bottom of my legs. I found an empty seat and sat there waiting for the movie to sort of sweep over me like movies usually do; but the whole time I was supposed to be watching the movie—which was one of those where they crash a car, hop

a runaway train, kill, kill, kill a person every three seconds—
I kept thinking about birthdays.

I thought about how, when you're a kid, everyone makes
a big deal out of your birthday, and I wondered if people
cared more about little kids or if there was some reason why
their birthdays are more important than adults'. I thought
about how everyone makes a big thing out of it when you're
little and you get in the habit of thinking your birthday is
important; then when you get older and no one does anything
about it, it's depressing as hell.

When I was a kid, I had the best birthday parties. My dad
would run around like a maniac making up games for us to
play. And my friends and I stuffed our faces with all kinds
of junk food. One kid always ate too much and threw up.
But, the best part was the goody bags. My mom and I would
go to the toy store and buy a whole bunch of ten-cent air-
planes, Super Balls, and plastic spiders, and pack these little
paper goody bags with the stuff. No other mother made
goody bags like mine. None, I swear.

After my dad left, I started having quieter parties. I don't
know if it was because he was gone or because I was getting
older. I mean, goody bags don't work too well for kids over
eight. My mom would say, "Invite five of your friends and
I'll take you all out to the movies and for pizza, or I'll buy
you and your best friends tickets to a basketball game." It
was nice of her to offer and all, but I could never figure who
to invite and who not to, and so I spent most of my birthdays
sitting at the kitchen table with my mother trying to convince
both of us that it would be better next year.

Right there in the movie theater, while Arnold Schwarzenegger was killing thirty million people, I made myself a

promise never to make a big deal out of my kid's birthdays. I figured the best thing to do is something small, something private, that you really enjoy, like going to a movie in the middle of the goddamned afternoon.

Later I snuck back to school and waited behind some parked cars for the final bell to ring. Michael drove up in his old VW, and even though it wasn't legal yet, he let me drive to the Motor Vehicle Administration.

I went to Window A, where I showed some lady my driver's-ed certificate and my birth certificate. She sent me over to Window B, where I got a form that I filled out while waiting in line at Window C.

Michael stood in the corner leaning against a wall, drinking a can of Coke.

After Window C, they sent me to Room 1, where I took the eye test. The eye machines were like those peep-show things that you drop seventy-five cents into and then get to watch about two minutes of a porno movie. I know I'm not supposed to know about those things, but I do. Max took me there a couple of times.

Anyway, I passed the vision test, twenty-twenty, and got sent to Room 2, which was down in the basement. By the time I got there, my palms were all sweaty and I had to keep wiping them on the thighs of my jeans.

A lady dressed like a cop, but definitely not a cop, handed me the test. I sat down in the very first chair. The room was flooded with fluorescent lights. They were too bright. I wondered how the lady cop could sit in there all day without having a nervous breakdown or something. I had to close my eyes for a couple of seconds. I opened them and looked down at the test. The paper seemed to reflect light, like a piece of aluminum foil on the beach, like the beach and the water, or something very bright like that.

I thought about what would happen if I failed the test. I would be the first person I knew to have had the chance to drive and completely screwed it up. I stopped thinking and started filling in the answers.

Question fourteen: If you are driving and an animal begins to cross your path, do you (a) swerve to avoid hitting the animal even if this means putting your vehicle or other vehicles in danger; (b) try to avoid the animal, but if you do strike it, move the animal to the side of the road and call the ASPCA; (c) blow your horn and flash your lights at the animal, hoping that this will scare him away; or (d) none of the above.

I answered b, even though I totally disagreed with them. It wasn't the time to stand up for my beliefs. After all, there was a fake lady cop sitting two feet in front of me, searching for signs that I wouldn't make a good driver. I signed the sworn statement, saying that I hadn't cheated or attempted to do anything illegal with their test, and gave the whole thing back to the cop.

She graded it right then and there. Ninety-six. She wouldn't tell me where I made my mistakes. She just said, "Congratulations, go upstairs." I went back up and got Michael.

"I got it," I said.

He didn't seem to hear me. He was sitting on a wooden bench, with a sort of glazed-over look. The Coke can was in his hands. He was bending it back and forth, trying to break it in half.

"I should never drink the stuff," he said. "I know better. Twelve teaspoons of sugar and caffeine. Picks you up and then drops you off a cliff."

"Did you get it?" my mom asked when we walked into the house.

"Sure did," Michael said. He was pretty well recovered by then.

My mom came out of the kitchen and hugged me. She got flour or something all over my shirt, then apologized, and then made it worse by trying to get the stuff off with her hands, which were covered in it in the first place.

"Can you get something down for me?" she asked.

I followed her into the kitchen. Just about every dish, plate, pot, whatever we had, was out.

"My white platter is up there," she said, pointing to the top shelf of the cabinet. "I think the roast would look right on a white platter. Meat always looks nice on white. I'll put some green stuff around it, some cherry tomatoes. What do you think?"

She was babbling on and on like a very weird person, but I didn't want to tell her that, because I figured she was nervous enough about the dinner and it seemed unfair to make her worry about going crazy just then, especially on my birthday.

"Fine," I said. I reached high, over my head, hooked the platter with two fingers, and pulled it down.

"Careful," my mom said, after the plate was already safely down.

"Anything else?" I asked.

"Michael's promised to do the vegetables. I've got the meat. Do you think we need bread? I could run over to the bakery."

"Relax," I said. "It'll be okay."

"I want it to be just right," she said.

It was obvious. In the middle of the night she was down there getting rid of the Kool-Aid stain.

"Did you see your cake?" Slowly she lifted the aluminum foil off the cake plate.

It was there, chocolate with at least an inch of icing, icing that could guarantee about five cavities per person. I wanted to run my fingers around the edge of the plate, just to get a little taste as a sort of an appetizer.

"I can't wait," I said.

"I have little plastic basketball-player decorations, but I thought I should ask you first."

"They're okay," I said, looking at the little plastic guys, with sharp things like spears attached to the bottoms of their shoes. "But do we have to actually put them on the cake? I'm getting kind of old for decorations."

"Are you?" She put the decorations back in a drawer.

I pulled the fake diamond from the playground out of my pocket and handed it to her. I really probably should have given it to Maggie or something, but I didn't know how she'd take it. I mean, I didn't want to make her think it was a serious thing or that I was too cheap to buy her a regular ring if I wanted to.

"Thanks," my mom said, actually putting the ring on her finger.

"Are you going to wear it?"

"Why not?"

"It's not real or anything."

"So what? I like it," she said. "Jack."

She paused, and I was afraid. I don't know why, but I thought she might say she couldn't go through with the dinner, she couldn't have my dad and Bob and everyone over at the house.

"What?" I said.

"Do me a favor." She paused again.

I hate it when people start to say something and then stop. The suspense kills me even if it's only a regular conversation.

"Look in the dining room."

I walked through the kitchen and into the dining room. We hardly ever spent any time in there. She'd set the table very fancy, like for a major dinner party.

"What?" I asked.

"Does it bother you that I folded the napkins so they look like flowers?"

"Should it?" I said.

My mother shook her head. "Jack," she said in the same voice as before.

I got scared. In fact, I got more scared. "What?"

"Look at the ceiling. It's peeling," she said. "I almost asked Michael to paint it, but the paint probably wouldn't dry quick enough and the whole place would smell."

I had to cut her off to keep her from going insane.

"No one is going to look up at the ceiling and notice that one small place is cracking. And even if they do . . ."

"Don't let Bob sit over there, okay. It might chip off while we're eating and fall into his plate."

"Mom, calm down, please. You're making me feel really weird."

"Maybe we should eat buffet style, in the living room. I could set up little trays?"

"Mom!" I yelled.

Michael came downstairs. "Don't fight," he said. "It's bad karma."

"We're not fighting," I said. "It's only a dinner," I told my mother. "It's only Dad."

She took a deep breath and opened the bottle of wine they were planning on drinking for dinner.

"Mom."

"It has to aerate, Jack," she said. "The wine has to get some air in it." She poured herself a small glass and put the roast in the oven.

◇   ◇   ◇

My dad and Bob showed up at exactly seven o'clock, give or take ten minutes. Whatever the hell time it was didn't matter, because we weren't ready.

My mom and Michael were going crazy in the kitchen, like French chefs about to make their grand debut. They kept crashing into each other and yelling that the kitchen wasn't big enough. I felt like a major irreversible disaster was about to happen.

Just as I opened the front door and said, "Hi, Dad," my mom yelled, "Oh, shit," from the kitchen.

Bob and my dad looked at each other in a funny way, like if they turned around real fast, got into their car, and went home, maybe no one would ever know they'd been there. No one except me.

"Come in," I said, standing a little bit away from the door, giving them room.

"Happy birthday," Bob said, stepping in and jamming a small wrapped box into my hand.

"Thanks," I said.

"Happy birthday, kiddo," my dad said, hugging and kissing me.

I kind of patted him on the back and mumbled. My mom came out of the kitchen, wiping her hands on a dish towel.

"Hi, Bob and Paul," she said as though she'd been re-hearsing it all day.

Hi, Bob and Paul, she said like it was a foreign language and she'd been practicing how to pronounce it just right.

Then, in one of those fake hostessy moves, she kissed my dad on the cheek, and he had to kiss her back. For a second it looked like she might do the same thing to Bob, but a fast, confused look went across her face, and I could completely see what she was thinking. She just looked at Bob and said, "Can I take your coat?"

Bob handed her the raincoat. If people could see I was thinking before I said anything, I'd buy a ski mask.

"Come in—sit down," my mother said, sweeping everyone into the living room. "Can I get you a drink?"

"Scotch," Bob said.

My mother looked over at my father. "Juice?" she asked. He nodded.

Michael came out with a big fruit, cheese, and cracker platter that he'd been putting together for the past half hour.

"Hi," he said, and then sat down on the sofa next to Bob because my dad was sitting in his old chair, the chair that was Michael's now.

My mom went back into the kitchen, and we all sat there eating, drinking, and kind of mumbling at one another. Every now and then, my mother would scream something like, "Goddamn it," and either Michael or I would go running in to see what'd happened.

"So you're going to get your license soon?" Bob said to me, and I nodded. "Do you like it?"

I wasn't sure whether getting a license was one of those things that you have the option of liking or not. I mean, it seemed like something you just do.

"I like to drive," I said.

"When I was sixteen," Bob said, "my friend Walker and I bought an old car and drove it all over hell and back. Never fixed it up or anything, just drove it with a big crash in the side, hardly any brakes, no horn, nothing. Then one night in the middle of the highway, it died. We coasted over to the side of the road, got out, and left the car right there, with the headlights on and everything, and walked the rest of the way home."

"I probably won't be getting a car for a while," I said.

"A long while," my dad said.

The doorbell rang, and I got up to let the Burkas in.

"Happy birthday, happy birthday, happy birthday," Sammy said, over and over again until I thought I'd have to grab him by the neck to make him stop.

"Oh, and by the way," Max said as soon as Sammy shut up, "happy birthday."

"Happy birthday, Jack," Mrs. Burka said, and I really wished it wasn't my birthday anymore.

"Hi," I said.

The bruises on her face were getting better. They were more orange and green than purple.

"Here," Max said, handing me a big flat box. "It's a present," Max said.

Mrs. Burka put her hand on Sammy's head and steered him into the living room. She seemed more relaxed and older. I couldn't figure out if Mr. Burka leaving made her feel more relaxed, at least knowing she wasn't going to get beat up anymore, and then by relaxing maybe her face kind of fell a little bit. You know, like muscles do when you just let them drop.

"Jack," my mom called from the kitchen. I went in to her.

"Is everything okay? Is everything working, out there?"

"Yeah," I said. "You should go out and have a drink with them. I'll stay here and watch everything."

I poured a little more wine into her glass and pointed her toward the living room.

"Don't let the string beans get well-done," she said.

I pushed her out of the kitchen and in with Mrs. B. and Michael.

My dad was busy taking Bob on a tour of the house. "This is where I had my first garden," I heard him say. "And this is where I used to play with Jack. We had a swing set here. I wonder what they did with it."

Gave it to the Salvation Army, I wanted to say, just like that damn lamp you borrowed from my room before you moved out. But it wasn't true. We tried to give it to the Salvation Army, but they wouldn't take it—too big, too rusty. We had to pay to have it hauled away.

Hearing my father tell Bob stuff like, "In the downstairs bathroom, I used to have a darkroom," made me feel like I was trapped in a historic landmark, like Mount Vernon or something.

It seemed like there should be a sign on the front door designating our house as important to the history of the world, protecting it from destruction or further alteration on account of the fact that Jack's dad used to live there. There should be a brass plaque outside with the dates my dad actually lived there across the top, and under that, a paragraph telling all about my dad, me, and our family.

Max came into the kitchen. "Where's Maggie? Is she coming?"

"She's late," I said.

And all of a sudden, I was in a bad mood. I wanted to go

up to my room, alone, and shut the door. But then when I thought about being up there, with my mom, Max, Mrs. Burka, Sammy, Michael, my dad, and Bob downstairs, I felt like running out of the house, into the woods, and hiding under a big tree for a long time, maybe forever.

"How come you're sitting in here?" Max said. He leaned against the counter and nearly knocked my mother's white platter over. "It's your birthday."

"I'm watching the food," I said.

I lifted the cover from the string beans and blew a cloud of steam into Max's face. He stepped back. I pulled one bean out and bit into it. They were getting too well-done.

"Mom," I yelled into the living room. She came running in like maybe I'd exploded the stove or something.

"What?" she said.

"The beans are done."

"Find your father. Tell him dinner's ready." She turned the light under the beans off and pulled the roast out of the oven.

"But Maggie's not here yet," I said.

"Jack," my mom said in that voice that mothers have, the voice that tells you it's not up for discussion.

I found my dad and Bob upstairs in my bedroom. They were standing there, and my dad was showing Bob all my stuff. "Dinner's ready," I said.

I wasn't thrilled to catch them there. I mean, if *I* wanted to show Bob my stuff, that was one thing; but parents definitely should not take their friends or whatevers into their kids' rooms.

I was tempted to say, This isn't a goddamned historic landmark. This is my life. I still live here. But I figured I should save it for later, for a day when it wasn't my birthday anymore.

I closed my door after they went out and wished I had a padlock or something.

When I got back downstairs, Maggie was just coming through the door. "Sorry I'm late," she said.

And then, in front of everyone, she kissed me. I liked that; besides the fact that it felt good, it was impressive. It meant I was making actual progress.

"My dad got home late," she said.

"What an asshole," Max said, and everyone looked at him like he was insane, but no one said anything.

"Anyway, this is for you," Maggie said.

She handed me a book. I mean, she handed me a present all wrapped up and everything, but I could tell in advance that it was a book.

"Thanks," I said.

"We have to eat now," my mother announced.

"Am I really late?" Maggie asked me.

"Not really," I said.

"Jack, you sit at the head of the table," my mom said. "And Maggie, next to Jack. And then Max, next to Maggie."

It worked out just right. Max, who never looked at anything other than food, especially during a meal, was right there under the cracked part of the ceiling, and my dad and Bob were clear over on the other side of the table just in case my mother's nightmare came true.

Every two seconds my mom jumped up to get something from the kitchen, or to check and see that she hadn't forgotten anything. At first, it made everyone uptight, and we sat there eating fast and kind of looking around at one another, but then both Mrs. B. and Michael told my mom to calm the hell down, and my dad complimented her fifty thousand times on the food, and by the time we were having seconds, she was sitting for at least five minutes in a row.

"These string beans are really special," Bob said. "What did you do to them?"

"We grew them," Michael said.

"Just a little lemon juice," my mom said.

"That must be it," Bob said. "We really ought to have a garden."

"You have to live in a house in order to have a garden," my dad said.

And while everyone was busy eating their string beans and roast beef, I looked around the table. It was as though everything I knew about each person flashed up on a screen above their heads, one at a time. As I sat there watching them chew, I felt worse and worse.

I went all the way around the table taking apart everyone's life. I thought about where they'd been, all that had happened, and where they were going. I even did it to Sammy. And when I got back to myself, I realized that I didn't want any part of it.

I don't mean that all of a sudden I was Mr. Wonderful and they were dirt. I just knew that I wanted something else, something different, something more. What made me feel totally suicidal right there at my birthday table was that I couldn't begin to say what the hell it was that I wanted.

My father pushed his plate away, leaned back in his chair, and stretched. "That was sooo good," he said, just like he'd said all the time, a million years ago, when he lived there and ate there every night.

When the eating part was over, everyone except me seemed more normal. My father took off his shoes and left them under the table, just like he used to. And everyone sat around talking just like a regular family.

"Do you know, Jack," my dad said. He wasn't talking to me exactly—it was more like he was talking about me but wanted to make sure I heard it.

"The very first night you came home from the hospital, I sat in your room, all night, just watching you."

Mrs. Burka made a sound, as if to say, How touching, and in a way it annoyed me.

My dad was playing with the wax around the edge of a candle, rolling it back and forth between his fingers.

"I sat upstairs in that room all night, simply looking," he said, and all the adults nodded, as if all of them were saying, That's so sweet. I felt a little sick to my stomach—too sweet.

"And then you were too tired to go to work the next morning," my mom said.

"He still doesn't like to get up and go to work," Bob said. "Some days, I have to practically drag him out of bed."

Max piled all of my presents onto the table and kind of forced me to open them; I was hoping to wait until later, until after everyone left. I hate opening presents in public. It makes me nervous as hell. I'm always afraid I'll have the wrong reaction to what's inside the box, and everyone will hate me or something.

Anyway, I had to open the stuff, so I tried to be cool about it. Luckily, no one got me anything too upsetting.

Maggie gave me a book. Books are always a good, intelligent gift, but she acted all embarrassed that it wasn't something more exciting and kept apologizing all over the place, even when I told her it was one I'd been dying to read, which wasn't really true.

Mrs. Burka had knitted me a big, thick sweater, which totally amazed me, no joke. No one ever made me a piece of clothing before, unless you count Halloween costumes. I put it on right away, even though it was about eighty degrees in the house.

My dad and Bob got me a camera, thirty-five millimeter, the real thing. As soon as I opened it, my dad started saying stuff about setting up a darkroom again. Then, he and Bob got into a mini-argument about where, considering that they only have one bathroom, and my dad said something about converting it into the darkroom.

"Great," Max said. "You can take porno pictures, develop them yourself, and we can sell them."

"Max, you seem like someone who might benefit from a little therapy," Bob said. And even though it was probably true, everyone was horrified that Bob actually said it. I mean, it was kind of harsh.

"What he really needs is a girlfriend," Mrs. B. whispered, loud enough for everyone to hear. And somehow Maggie and I both got embarrassed.

Michael and my mom got me a telephoto zoom lens to go with the camera.

"We worked together on this one," she said, smiling at my dad, who smiled back at her. It seemed a little forced but not too bad.

Then my mom brought the cakes out of the kitchen. Her cake first, with about two thousand blazing candles. She put it down in front of me and ran back to get the cake my dad had brought from the bakery, the cake that said HAPPY BIRTH-DAY, JACK in big blue letters.

I blew the candles out, and everyone started singing that

song—you know which one—and I felt like hiding under the table. I felt like completely revoking my birthday.

Max and Sammy added the extra verse about looking like a monkey and acting like one, too, so it took awhile.

"Thanks," I said. "Thanks a lot."

Thanks is a wonderful word because you can use it even when you don't mean it and usually people can't tell the difference.

Anyway, we ate cake, my mom's cake. I tried a piece of the other one just to make sure my dad didn't feel left out. Compared to my mother's, the bakery cake tasted like plastic frosting sprayed onto a bunch of sponges dipped in sugar.

I guess the whole dinner thing went okay. Nothing fell on anyone, and no one choked to death or anything, so I figure that was good.

◇   ◇   ◇

When everything was over—the wrapping paper all balled up in the trash and the ribbons turned into jewelry for Sammy—Max, Maggie, and I went out for a walk. I would rather have gone alone, but there was no way I could desert everyone.

As soon as we got outside, Max lit up a cigarette, his latest disgusting habit. Maggie slipped her hand into mine, and we walked.

"Do you ever look at your family and get nauseous?" I asked. "I mean, do you ever think about how you don't want to end up like them and then get scared that it's already too late, that you're already exactly the same as them?"

"Just because it's your birthday doesn't mean you have to turn into Mr. Philosophical," Max said.

"Do you look at them and think maybe you could leave and come back in five years and everything would be the same?"

"No," Max said.

Maggie squeezed my hand and kissed the side of my face. "Don't worry," she said.

I wasn't worried. I was totally freaking out. I thought about how everyone always told me I could be whatever I wanted, that all I had to do was decide what it was and go after it. It was the go-after-it part I was just beginning to understand. I'd always believed them. I liked the idea that I could be anything, that I should be who I was and not who someone else thought I should be.

But just then, out walking with Max and Maggie, I realized it was all up to me, that I had to do whatever it was I wanted, and just deciding was the easy part. I mean, I realized I actually had to go out and do *it*, whatever *it* was.

All the stuff about my mom and dad, and Michael and Bob, didn't seem quite as important. I don't mean I didn't care about them or didn't think about my dad being gay anymore. I thought about it all the time, and to be honest, it still didn't completely make sense. The thing was, whatever he or any of them were or weren't didn't really have anything to do with me. We were all separate. I only wished I'd known it a couple of years ago.

I'm Jack, that's all. I'm Jack, just Jack out there by myself. And I know it sounds stupid and obvious and all that, but I didn't really understand it until just then, and even then I wasn't sure I understood it completely.

When we got back to the house, I wanted to go upstairs and lock myself into a room until a couple of years went by and some of this stuff disappeared. I wanted to lock myself away until everything didn't seem like such an emergency anymore.

But I couldn't do it. I couldn't, because Mrs. Burka and my mom were in the kitchen drying pots and pans, my dad and Michael were playing chess, and Bob was complaining. I couldn't do it with a million people sitting around celebrating my birthday.

"Try to hurry," Bob kept saying. "I'm very tired. Tomorrow's a workday for me."

"Okay, okay," my dad said, bumping one of Michael's pawns off the board.

"We really should go," Mrs. B. said after the dishes were dried. "It's late for Sammy."

"No," Sammy said.

I think he was going through a delayed no phase. Suddenly, at five and a half, he was acting like a two-year-old.

"We should go, too," my dad said as Michael won their game. "Jack, how about a little driving practice tomorrow?"

"I need to parallel park," I said. I needed a lot of things, but that was the simplest.

"I'll pick you up at ten-thirty," he said.

"Thanks for having us," Bob said as my mom got him his raincoat.

"We can drop Maggie," Mrs. Burka said.

I stood there in a daze, nodding, and thanking everyone.

"You're growing up," my dad said, hugging me one more time.

I was tempted to tell him that I hadn't even started yet.

They all walked across the lawn toward the cars. I watched them leave, then closed the door and locked it.

"Come sit," my mom said, patting a place next to her on the sofa. She wrapped her arms around me.

Michael was in the dining room, taking the tablecloth off, putting out the candles, cleaning up.

"It was nice tonight," she said. "Your father seems happy with Bob."

"I think he is," I said. "Do you think Mrs. Burka looks older?"

"Things are hard. I think Sandy wants Max to come and live with him. There may be a custody fight."

We were quiet for a long time.

"I feel like I'm starting to lose you," she said.

I couldn't answer her.

"There's no way to stop you, is there?"

"Thanks for the party," I said. "It was really nice. A real birthday." I picked up my presents and stuff and started to go upstairs. "I mean, the food was wonderful, everyone seemed to have a good time, and the paint didn't fall on anyone."

Michael came out of the kitchen and sat down next to my mom. He picked up her feet and started massaging them.

"It was nice," she said. I started up the steps to my room. " 'Night," she said.

"Happy birthday, kiddo," Michael said.

I went up to my room, planning to sit there until I got old. But about two seconds later, I picked up my old basketball and went back downstairs.

"I'll be back in a little while. I need some air, some exercise."

"Watch out for your leg," my mom said.

I walked down the street toward the park. I walked down

the sidewalk bouncing the ball, never sure exactly where it would land and where it would come up next.

I walked through the night thinking. It wasn't like I wanted to think. Half the reason I was out there was because I wanted to stop thinking. But thinking isn't always something you can control. Like Michael says, Go with it. I mean, if you're thinking stuff you don't want to think and you try and stop, it only gets worse, so I figured why the hell not think straight through it.

Okay, so I knew I was Jack, all alone. Jack singular. I don't mean that all of a sudden I was an orphan or anything. I would always be my mother's Jack, and my father's Jack, and the Jack with the gay father and Bob, and the Century 21 mom and Michael, Max and Mrs. B. I would always be all that, but more than anything I was plain Jack, no strings attached.

Don't think it was something that had to do with getting my learner's permit and all of a sudden having a whole lot of freedom. Michael's favorite singer, Janis Joplin, had this whole bit about how "Freedom's just another word for nothing left to lose," and besides the fact that I never agreed with her, it just wasn't like that. All this stuff had nothing to do with driving or being free. In fact, it was almost the opposite of being free; it was a full-time job.

I stopped bouncing the ball and just held it in my hands, sometimes throwing it up in the air, spinning it backward, and then catching it again. I'd already gotten pretty far, in the sense that at least I knew what the game was, what was really going on. And guys like Max—well, it seemed like proof positive that the age of the family had peaked and was currently on the downhill trail. I'm not trying to say that families are for shit or anything, but stuff was changing and I knew it, and I felt good about knowing because it seemed like maybe by knowing I'd be able to do something different and not have the same damned thing happen to me.

I realize I'm all over the place and mumbling like hell. But that's how it was. I was walking, playing catch with myself, and trying to figure out the whole world and still be home before the goddamned eleven-o'clock news. What I'm really trying to say is that while I was out there walking, I got a grip. I knew there was a chance.

Right near the park the sidewalk curved and kind of hovered on a skinny little hill just above the road. I stopped playing with the ball and just carried it, pressed into my hip. I carried it because I figured that with one wrong bounce, it would probably end up under the wheels of some old guy's station wagon.

Anyway, I crossed the street and went into the park. It was dark on account of the path lights having been disconnected during one of the energy crises and no one ever bothering to come up with a new way to see in the dark. I wished I'd brought a flashlight. I got spooked as hell when I heard something crunching behind me. I turned around fast, like if it was a monster or a boogeyman I'd scare him back. I turned around fast and saw a raccoon going through a trashcan.

"Thanks a lot, mister," I said, giving it one of Max's get-lost looks.

The courts were invisible except for the hoops, which were outlined by the light spilling over from the tennis courts. I put four quarters into the light box and bought a half hour of full-court bright white light.

I stood in the middle and tried to get started. When you're

out there alone, under the bright white, it's a little hard to get going. It's like being up on the high dive and all of a sudden wondering why you're there. But once I was really out there moving, dancing down the court, I remembered what it was all about. I was sharp; my mind was flowing. I dribbled, slamming the ball down with the tips of my fingers. The sound echoed like a slap against the little house where they sold refreshments during the day. I was out there, I was playing, I was Fast Jack, and I knew I would be okay, permanently. Right there on the basketball court, I knew I would make it.

I went charging down the court, shouting in great war whoops. I went charging down, bouncing the ball high like a little kid. At half-court, I stopped and heaved the ball toward the goal. Under the lights I could see it spinning backward, the stripes running together, turning into a thin black line. The light box clicked off and the court dropped into a blackness that seemed darker than the night, and I heard the ball go whooshing through the metal net.